MYSTERY AT [illegible] E

Ja[illegible]

First published in 2010 as a Kindle e-book

Cover design by Vanessa Burger

Author's website
www.just4kix.jimdo.com

RUNNER-UP IN THE PAN MCMILLAN 2010 YA NOVEL COMPETITION

MYSTERY at Ocean Drive

JAN HURST-NICHOLSON

www.just4kix.jimbo.com

Also by Jan Hurst-Nicholson

But Can You Drink The Water?

The Breadwinners

With the Headmaster's Approval

I Made These Up (short stories for the fireside)

Something to Read on the Plane

For Children
by
Janet Hurst-Nicholson

The Race (an inspiring story for left-handers)

Bheki and the Magic Light

Leon Chameleon PI and the case of the missing canary eggs

Leon Chameleon PI and the case of the kidnapped mouse

Jake

For my parents
Bill and Pat

1

If Jason had brought his motorbike to a stop before reaching into his delivery bag for a newspaper his life would have been very different that summer.

As the black Mercedes swept out of the driveway Jason and the driver saw each other at almost the same moment. Jason hit the scrambler's brakes and swung it into a desperate swerve, but the back wheel locked and he went into a skid. He flew through the air and smacked into the towering brick gatepost before landing with a wallop on the grass verge. He watched helplessly as the scrambler slewed beneath the wheels of the car, which screeched to a stop with a smell of burning rubber.

The rear door flew open and a teenage girl scrambled out. Jason found himself looking into an attractive sun-brown face. Silky black hair fell about her face and framed hazel eyes wide with concern.

"Are you all right?" She had a trace of an accent.

"I think so," he managed, reddening when he realised how stupid he must look with blood oozing from his elbow and knee, and his nose and cheeks lit up by blobs of fluorescent green sun block. He'd come straight from the beach and was going back after his paper round.

Tossing the hair from her face, she knelt to help him. He caught her staring at his T-shirt, the front of which was emblazoned `HELP A HORNY FRIEND'. He was about to explain about the rhino foundation when a middle-aged woman leapt from the car and roughly took the girl's arm.

"Tessa," she hissed, yanking the girl back into the car.

Angry words were exchanged in a language Jason didn't recognise. The woman's harsh angry screech, and the short dark hair scraped back from her face reminded Jason of a crow.

The driver had retrieved the scrambler from beneath the car's wheels and was busy examining the Merc's bodywork for damage. Powerfully built with a square head and droopy black moustache, he looked like an irate pirate as he checked the car's underside. Satisfied that there was no damage he turned his angry attention to Jason.

"Look where you're going next time. This is an expensive car." His heavy accent matched his glowering face.

Jason spluttered a protest, but it was brushed aside as the man turned and climbed back behind the steering wheel. The massive wooden gates swished closed and the car purred off, leaving Jason to struggle to his feet.

The girl was peering through the back window. As their eyes met he was sure she mouthed "Help". Stunned, he raised his hand to acknowledge that he'd understood, but when she tried to wave back the woman put a restraining hand on her arm. He was still staring after the car as it rounded the corner of Ocean Drive and sped towards the freeway.

He stood for a long moment puzzled at the odd and rude behaviour of the older couple. Who was this Tessa and why didn't they want him to speak to her? Did she really ask for help? Had she been kidnapped? If he was wrong, it wouldn't be the first time his imagination had got him into trouble. Still wondering, he bent to pick up his precious scrambler. A searing spasm shot through his right shoulder and he gasped in pain. He must have wrenched it when he collided with the gatepost. Gingerly he moved his arm. Nothing seemed to be broken or dislocated. He gently rubbed his shoulder. He would have to lay off volleyball and surfing for a few days.

A quick check of the scrambler revealed a bent surfboard carrier and deep scratches in the red paint of the petrol tank, but there didn't appear to be any serious damage. He threw his leg over the seat and kicked the starter. The engine spluttered and died. He tried again and this time it burst into life. He let out the throttle, and forgoing his usual wheelie start, set off at a sedate pace to finish his paper round. He winced as he tossed the papers over the high walls and railings that bordered most of the properties on his round. No point in going back to the beach with a painful shoulder. He would head for home and check the computer printout of his deliveries. He was anxious to know who lived at number 69 Ocean Drive.

From what he'd been able to see over the high brick wall he knew it was a double-storey house, almost palatial in size, with a portico over the front door. The rear would back onto the beach, as did all the houses on that side of the road. Only the very wealthy could afford to live on Ocean Drive. Perhaps that was why they didn't want Tessa associating with a newspaper boy.

He was dabbing the grazes on his arm with a dampened kitchen towel when his sister came in.

"What happened to you?"

He explained about the sudden appearance of the car. "But don't tell Mom," he warned. "I'll tell her I was dumped, surfing."

"D'you think that'll make her feel any better?" Caitlin gave him a rueful smile.

"I'd rather she confiscated my surfboard than my scrambler." He grinned back.

"Here," said Caitlin, reaching into the cupboard for the antiseptic cream. "Let me put some of this on."

"Ouch." He winced, smarting from the pain.

"That should do it." Caitlin was used to bandaging up her younger brother. "But you'd better wear a long-sleeved shirt on Saturday."

"Saturday?"

"Jaasonnn," she threatened. "You can't have forgotten. You and Mark promised to be waiters at that 25th wedding anniversary I'm catering."

"Cait," groaned Jason. He didn't mind helping with twenty-firsts and matric parties where there were young people and decent music, but wedding anniversaries were a real bore. Old people were embarrassing when they got tiddly.

"Come on, Jason. I thought you needed the money," Caitlin coaxed.

That was true. The model helicopter he and his Dad were building was proving very expensive. His newspaper money wouldn't even cover the cost of the motor.

"What time do you want us there?" he sighed.

"No later than seven. I want everything to go smoothly. It's important. I'm still relying on word of mouth for business. It's not easy when you start your own catering firm." Then she added pointedly, "And make sure Mark's wearing decent shoes this time, and not those tatty trainers."

"Okay." He reached into the fridge for a slice of leftover pizza. He took it to his bedroom and ate it hungrily while he flipped through the computer printout of his round. The list was printed according to road names. He soon found Ocean Drive. Number 69 was listed as Wilson. J. There was even a telephone number. He tore some paper out of an old maths book and jotted down the number.

He was standing in the hallway with the telephone receiver in his hand when he realised he had no idea what he was going to say. "Hello Tessa, I'm Jason, the idiot who fell off his bike?" He needed a genuine reason to call. Then he remembered the newspaper. He must have thrown 69's over the wall because he did not have any papers left at the end of his round, but Tessa wouldn't know that. He would ask if they had got it.

He started to punch in the numbers, but noticed that for some odd reason his mouth felt dry. He didn't know why. He'd dated plenty of girls. What was so different about this one?

But when he had finished dialling, all he got was the prolonged bleep of a discontinued number. Blast. He dialled Directory Enquiries and a bored voice told him the Wilson's number had been cancelled the previous month.

He tried the subscription department of the newspaper and after an interminable wait he learned that the Wilsons had paid an eighteen-month subscription in advance and had not bothered to ask for a rebate when they left. It would run through to the middle of next year.

There did not seem much else he could do right then. However, tomorrow he would ring the bell at number 69 and ask to speak to Tessa. If the family were new to the neighbourhood he would offer to show Tessa around. If she really did need help, she would tell him.

Mark arrived as they were finishing supper. "Want a Coke?" Jason handed him the bottle.

Mark fetched a glass. He knew Jason's kitchen almost as well as his own.

The boys carried their drinks to the workshop that Jason's father had made at the back of the garage. Jason stepped over the untidy jumble hardly noticing the mess. The shelves were crammed with solar film, model kits, ailerons, engines and drawers marked SERVOS, SPINNERS, SILENCERS, PROPELLERS. There were clear plastic drawers filled with numerous unidentified plastic and metal objects. Propped up against one wall was a graveyard of smashed planes, evidence of the years that Jason and his father had devoted to their hobby. Their latest project - a Jet Ranger helicopter - was standing on the bench amidst tubes of glue, tins of epoxy, drills, heat guns and tiny nuts, bolts and screws. Close-by, next to a dust-coated portable TV, hung three radio control transmitters.

Mark scuffed his feet through the drifts of balsa shavings. "Don't you ever lose anything in this mess?"

"Sometimes," admitted Jason. "But if it's anything metal we usually find it with Dad's electric magnet."

"Is your Dad away again?"

"Yeh, be back Friday night. I promised I'd have this rotor working by then." He found a screwdriver in a drawer and began tightening screws.

Mark noticed the grazes on Jason's elbow. "Fell off the scrambler, eh. Another corner you couldn't handle?"

"Get lost, Mark. It wasn't my fault." He jabbed Mark with the screwdriver.

"What happened?"

Jason told him the story. "And you know what? I think there's something wrong. Tessa could be in trouble."

"Tessa," mimicked Mark. "On first name terms, eh."

"Come on Mark, I'm serious."

"A hot chick, heh." Mark took a length of balsa from a box and made slashing sword swipes at Jason. "A fair damsel in distress. Prince Valiant to the rescue."

"Watch you don't break that," warned Jason, ignoring the jibe. "Balsa wood's not cheap."

Mark tossed the wood back into the box. "Hey, Jase, lighten up. You've been watching too many detective movies. You can't honestly think she needs rescuing? It's just an excuse to get to know her."

"Something didn't seem right."

"Remember the `dead body' you saw in that car. Turned out to be a shop dummy," Mark reminded him, grinning.

No one would ever let him forget that. An active imagination did have its drawbacks. But this was different, he was sure of it. "She seemed scared."

"That's not exactly evidence of a kidnapping. How scared did she look? Was she hurt - bruises or anything?"

"No," admitted Jason.

"So what made you think something was wrong?"

"The look in her eyes as they drove off. I'm sure she asked for help. And the way they hurried her away, as if they didn't want me to see her."

"Have you looked in the mirror lately?" Mark grunted and made gorilla faces.

"Wise guy, heh." Jason plucked a screw from the mess on the bench and slipped it into a hole on the rotor blade. He was thinking about the child in England who had been murdered and how the witnesses had regretted not acting on their suspicions. "I'm going to speak to her and ask her outright if everything is okay."

"Let me know your mystery lady's answer," teased Mark.

Jason threw a glue-encrusted rag at him. Mark ducked and the rag caught an empty bottle on the end of a shelf. He leapt to catch it, but he was too late and it smashed on the floor."

"No wonder the school didn't want you for the cricket team."

"Now if it had been a volleyball..." said Mark, picking up the shards of glass and dropping them in a bin.

"Are you playing tomorrow?"

"Probably in the afternoon. I'm working at my Dad's in the morning. He's got some more electronic components he wants stripping. You never know, I might be able to make another computer from the stuff they chuck away. Are you going down to the beach?"

"Maybe, later on. I wrenched my shoulder. I'll watch. Besides, I want to do some more work on the chopper."

"Do you really think all this model building is going to help you get into the airforce?" He knew Jason's life-long ambition was to be a pilot.

"I reckon that knowing how a plane operates will help," said Jason. "Take this chopper. The same number and type of controls are needed with this as with a full-sized chopper. If anything, a model is more difficult to fly because you are not sitting inside it and you can't feel its movements, and compensate. And with a model plane, you sometimes can't tell whether it's flying towards you or away from you."

"You can never tell whether you're coming or going anyway," laughed Mark.

"Ha, ha. Very funny."

Mark watched Jason adjust the fibreglass blades until they were balanced. They joked and chatted while he worked, until Mark, who did not have Jason's patience, became bored and decided it was time to go.

"See you tomorrow," he said. "Give my love to your new lady friend. Don't get too carried away!" He blew kisses as he darted out of the door.

Jason sprinted after him down the driveway. "See'ya," he called as Mark swung his scrambler out of the gate and roared off with a cheery wave.

The following morning after breakfast Jason busied himself with the Jet Ranger. He was hoping his father would have had time to pick up some inflatable floats they would use as a sort of training undercarriage to cushion the framework if they made a rough landing. Although he was quite proficient with choppers it still took a while to get used to a new model. But Tessa was never far from his mind.

Later that day he set off to collect the newspapers for his delivery.

Ocean Drive was about halfway through his round and he timed it so he would arrive at the same time as the previous day. Perhaps Tessa's outings were a regular occurrence. This time he was more careful as he approached number 69.

He stopped the bike and cut the engine. There was an intercom on the gatepost. He pressed the button. There was no buzzing sound or indication that it was working. However, after a while he heard a muffled, “Yes.” It sounded like a woman's voice. Maybe it was the crow.

"May I speak to Tessa, please?"

There was a long silence, and then a man asked abruptly, "Who are you?"

"Jason. Jason Hunter. I deliver the newspapers. I met Tessa yesterday when I fell off my bike. May I speak to her please."

"You must have the wrong house. There's no Tessa here."

Jason frowned. "The young girl in the black Mercedes. She was here yesterday."

"There's no young girl here."

Jason heard the click as the receiver was replaced.

2

Something was very wrong. Why would they deny that Tessa had ever been there? Jason stood for a moment chewing his lip and wondering what to do next. He had to find some way of contacting Tessa. Perhaps the neighbours had heard something. But he could hardly ask them straight out. Then he remembered that the newspaper encouraged the boys to find new subscribers.

The house opposite looked a good prospect, and the heavy metal gates were open. He wheeled the scrambler across the road and propped it against the wall hoping it wouldn't leave drips of oil on the brickwork driveway. Pulling off his helmet he flicked his hair out of his eyes and made his way to the front door.

An elderly man answered the knock, a magazine in his hands. He peered at Jason over his glasses. No, he couldn't authorise a subscription. It was his daughter's house. Jason would have to come back later when she came home from work.

"You wouldn't know anything about the people across the road, would you?" An elderly man with nothing much to do might find an interest in the comings and goings of his neighbours.

"Moved in about a month ago. Lots of official-looking cars. It wouldn't surprise me if it wasn't something to do with the government." He tapped his nose as though he suspected a conspiracy.

"Did you hear any names mentioned?" persisted Jason.

"No, they're not very friendly round here. Not like the street where the wife and I lived. Thirty years we were there. Knew everyone."

"Thanks anyway." Jason made his goodbyes before the old man could get carried away with his reminiscences.

That line of questioning didn't get me very far he thought as he strode down the driveway. Glancing across at number 69 he sensed a movement in one of the upstairs rooms. He stopped and took a closer look. A figure was standing in the window watching him.

When he got nearer, he recognised Tessa. So, she WAS there. Those people were lying. He waved his helmet to let her know he had seen her. Suddenly another figure appeared. It was the crow. She snatched the curtains closed and Tessa was lost to view.

This was more mysterious than ever. He had to find out what was going on.

Perhaps Mark would believe him now. He clamped on his helmet and sped off to finish his round.

When he swung into the beach car park the guys were finishing a game of volleyball. He could see Mark's tall figure close to the net. The ball smashed towards him, too high for him to reach, thought Jason. But Mark would have a go at anything, something that did not always go down well with his partners, and he leapt like a young springbok. His arm came up like a whip, his elbow drawn back. His hand came into explosive contact with the ball and his wrist snapped it over the net in a hard-driven spike between the two unsuspecting opponents. There was a cheer and then a whistle shrilled the end of the game.

Smiling, Jason ran his fingers through his sun-blonde hair, which his helmet always managed to flatten, glad to feel the cool sea breeze on his head. A ghetto-blaster was belting out sixties ballads to a group of teenagers lazing on towels. He sprinted down the steps. As he ran onto the beach, a scream and shrieks came from the foaming waves that were pounding the shoreline and hissing up the beach.

Jason saw the looks of concern turn to sighs of resignation as Nicole, Mark's wacky younger sister laughingly recovered the bodyboard from which she had fallen. For years Mrs Boyd's instructions to him and Mark, "Now you two look after Nicole," had been a trial of patience. Tricky Nicky, they'd called her. Now that she was a teenager she hadn't improved, he thought ruefully.

Mark had spotted Jason and he and David jogged over. "How's it?" panted Mark, punching Jason on the arm.

"How's the new girlfriend?" said David, winking at Mark. "Still locked up in the castle waiting to be rescued?"

"Hah, very funny," said Jason. He turned to Mark. "I suppose you've told everyone."

"Only Dave." He grinned. "Did you manage to speak to Tessa?"

Jason filled them in on his latest encounter. "I saw her in the window. Why would they deny she's there?"

"There's probably a perfectly plausible reason," said Mark. He gave David a knowing look. "Perhaps they've heard about me and my effect on women. They're keeping her locked away."

David laughed. But he could see that Jason was genuinely concerned. "What are you going to do, Jase?"

"I'll have a look at the back of the house. Maybe there's a gate that leads onto the beach."

"But you can't just walk in," said David.

"I'll think of some excuse." Jason would not be put off. "Are you two coming?"

"I'm game," said Mark. "If she means this much to you after one meeting she must be a pretty hot chick. I'd like to meet her. Come on then."

They piled their towels and beach gear into their backpacks and slung them over their shoulders. David climbed onto the back of Mark's scrambler.

"It'll be quicker if we use the road," Jason said. "There's an open plot at the end of Ocean Drive which leads onto the beach. We'll leave the bikes there and walk." He kicked the starter and the engine burst into life, drowning Mark's reply.

The plot was overgrown but they found a pathway through the bush and were soon on the beach. The rear of many of the houses along Ocean Drive were hidden from view by the coastal vegetation, but in some places trees had been cut back to allow access to the beach. And there were dips in the dunes, which offered some of the homeowners splendid sea views. All the double-storey houses had sea views from their upper storeys.

The boys ambled along the beach keeping to the solid sand of the waterline which was easier than trudging through the soft dunes. Jason studied the roofs of the houses, trying to work out which was number 69. He recognised a Spanish-style villa, but he couldn't recall whether it had been five or six houses from number 69.

"It's a white house, double-storey and big," said Jason.

"That narrows it down to about seventy-five percent of the houses," said Mark. "Can't you remember the shape?"

"It'll look different from the back," Jason defended.

"Were there any trees you'd recognise? A Jacaranda or something?" David was a keen bird-watcher and consequently knew most of the trees and bushes in the area.

"I didn't recognise any trees," said Jason. "But what I do remember," he added, suddenly sprinting up the beach, "is the pattern on the top of this wall." There was a dip in the dunes that revealed a white-painted wall nearly two metres high with a type of Greek-key design on the top.

"Are you sure this is it?" Mark demanded.

"This is it."

They walked along the perimeter wall until they came to a gate. It was very new, solid wood. Jason tried the handle. It didn't even turn. "Must be bolted from the inside," he decided.

"Now what?" said Mark.

"If we move further back we might be able to see the upstairs rooms." Jason stood on one of the dunes. "Look, there's a balcony running the full length of the house. There are tables and chairs, and what looks like drinks' cabinet. They probably spend a lot of time out there."

"So would I." David had been watching a sand plover running along the water's edge.

That gave Jason an idea. "Hey, Dave. Have you got your binoculars?"

"Why?"

"Come on, Dave. Lend them to me."

David rummaged in his bag. "Be careful." They were new. He took them out of the case and gave the lenses a careful wipe with a cloth before handing them over.

Jason focused on the upper rooms. Two of them appeared to be bedrooms with French doors leading to the balcony, but the middle room had wide sliding doors. They were open and he could see cane furniture and a television. Obviously an informal lounge.

"This is going to take some explaining if they catch us spying on them," muttered David.

"We're bird-watching," said Jason.

"Yeah, but what kind of birds?" quipped Mark.

"Watch out," whispered David. Someone had come out of one of the bedrooms. They ducked behind a dune.

Jason zeroed in on the figure. "It's Tessa." She was carrying a pile of books. She dropped them on the table, pulled out a chair, and opened one of the books. "Looks like she's studying." He leapt up and waved.

"Be careful," warned David. "What if someone sees us?"

But Jason wasn't listening. Tessa had spotted them. She stood up and glanced round, evidently looking to see if anyone was watching.

"Mark," said Jason urgently, "have you got your cellphone?" Mark's parents had insisted he and Nicole both carry phones for emergencies because Mark's scrambler wasn't very reliable, and Nicole belonged to lots of clubs and groups and was always wanting lifts.

"It's in my bag. Why?"

"What's the number?" Jason grabbed a stick and scrawled his name in huge letters on the wet sand. As Mark recited the number Jason wrote it in the sand.

Mark took the binoculars and trained them on the balcony. "Wow, she's quite something," he said.

When Jason finished writing he waved Mark's phone at Tessa and pointed to the number on the sand.

She understood immediately. He saw her scribble down the number and slip inside.

When the phone rang Jason grinned and nodded to the other two. He said a nervous hello. But before he could get any further he recognised Tessa's voice urging him, "Jason, you've got to help me. Get in contact with my mother, her name's..." But she got no further. A click indicated the phone had been cut off.

"Get down," urged Jason, realising that someone must have been listening. The boys ducked behind the dune. Jason levelled the binoculars on the balcony. Sure enough the crow appeared. She looked searchingly round the garden before moving her attention to the beach. To his horror, Jason realised that his name and the telephone number were still visible in the wet sand. He held his breath. But his luck was in. It was high tide and a wave frothed up the beach. As it receded it took his name with it. The crow withdrew inside.

"That was close," said Jason, in a relieved breath.

"What did Tessa say?" asked David.

"She does need help. She wants me to contact her mother."

Mark's eyes rolled heavenward. "Oh, come on. That sounds a bit heavy. Aren't you getting carried away?"

"Who is her mother? What's her name?" David needed facts.

"That's just it. The phone was disconnected before she could tell me," said Jason grimly.

"So what are you going to do? Hope she phones again?" asked David.

"I don't think it's likely they'll let her anywhere near a phone after this," said Jason.

"I think we should go to the cops," said David.

"As if they'd believe you." Mark remembered the `body' in the car. "They'd laugh at us."

"No. Dave's right," agreed Jason. "She could be in danger. Perhaps we should tell the cops." He was more concerned than ever now that his suspicions had been confirmed. "Come on, let's go. The crow and her piratical buddy might decide to move Tessa somewhere else."

They sprinted back to the scramblers. Jason roared ahead, only slowing when he neared the police station.

A female officer was manning the long wooden counter. At the far end Jason could see a policeman shuffling papers, the corners lifted gently by the breeze from two whirling ceiling fans. From a passage a young policeman emerged carrying a tray with tea and biscuits. He knocked on a door, waited, and then disappeared behind it.

The wooden floor creaked as the boys approached the counter. When the female officer glanced up enquiringly Jason realised how foolish he was going to sound. As he began his story he could see the doubt starting to cloud her face. But he knew there were enough child abusers and paedophiles about for her not to ignore him completely. She made some notes as he talked and then went over to the radio. "Uniform Romeo Three. Do you copy?"

Jason heard the crackled reply. "Affirmative."

"Are you available?"

"Just finishing a housebreaking statement. I'll be available in about five mikes."

She glanced at the three boys as she spoke into the microphone. "When you've finished, please go to 69 Ocean Drive. Complaint of suspicious circumstances."

The radio crackled back. "What sort of suspicious circumstances?"

"The complainants are three young men. They think a teenage girl by the name of Tessa could be in some sort of trouble. D'you copy?"

Jason noted the long silence before Uniform Romeo Three replied. "Copy. Be there in about ten mikes."

The officer noted down Jason's particulars while Mark and David sat idly reading the posters warning about explosives and the dangers of drugs.

Jason joined them as an elderly man wearing baggy shorts came in to report the theft of a lawnmower. "I was only gone for a few minutes to answer the phone."

"I'm afraid a few minutes is all it takes," sighed the policewoman, smoothing the page in preparation for yet another set of particulars.

The radio crackled with several messages, but it was almost fifteen minutes before Uniform Romeo Three reported. "I interviewed the occupants. 69

Ocean Drive is the private residence of a South American Embassy. They say there are no teenagers staying there. Report all is in order."

"Thank you Uniform Romeo Three," replied the woman officer.

Jason couldn't believe it. How could the people at Ocean Drive tell such blatant lies? "But Tessa is there. We all saw her," he protested.

"I'm afraid we'll have to take their word for it. We have no authority to enter an embassy."

"But you've got to do something. She could be in danger."

"I'm sorry," said the officer.

"Can't you do anything?" he pleaded. It seemed incredible that the police were powerless to help.

"All we can do is report any suspicions to the embassy head. But in this case I don't think we have enough to warrant an official letter."

"Come on Jase, let's go," said Mark, his arm on Jason's shoulder. "You've done all you can."

"No I haven't," said Jason, his mouth set in a determined line.

3

On Friday Jason woke to bright spears of sunlight lancing his face through the wafting bedroom curtains. He felt groggy, and in those few seconds before becoming fully awake, unaccountably afraid. Crazy dreams, weird people and unspeakable tortures had punctuated his sleep. Then he remembered Tessa and knew that it was her he was afraid for. I can't just abandon her. And if the police have their hands tied, then it's up to me, he thought. He felt sure David would help, and Mark was always game, even if he was still a bit sceptical.

Jason spent the morning checking the radio receiver in the chopper, and ensuring the servos and push rods had been fitted correctly. One missing screw could mean its destruction. Not only would weeks of work be wasted, but it would also prove very expensive. However, Tessa was never far from his thoughts. He considered, and then discarded several plans for making contact with her.

When he had finished working on the chopper, he still hadn't come up with any concrete ideas. He threw a cheese and polony sandwich together and washed it down with a glass of Coke before heading for the beach where he knew he would find Mark and David.

The regular crowd was gathered at the usual spot near the lifeguards' lookout. He could see a few surfers drifting just beyond the breakers. He shaded his eyes looking for Mark, but the surfers were too far out.

A wave started curling close to the beach. A couple of bodyboarders caught it, but one mistimed and was pitched out as it broke. The other came streaking in on the wall of water. Someone yelled and a group cavorting at the water's edge scattered as the bodyboarder skidded up the beach. As soon as she stood up, Jason recognised Nicole. He waved. She saw him and sprinted across the hot sand. "Did you see that?" she panted, laughing as she shook the water out of her hair, oblivious to the fright she had given everyone. "I couldn't stop."

"You ought to be more careful. You should have flipped out." He still felt like a big brother. "You could have mown someone down."

"They know to get out of my way." She laughed, flashing the brilliant smile that always managed to keep her out of serious trouble.

"Remind me to stay clear in a couple of years when you start learning to drive," said Jason.

"You mean you're not going to teach me?" She looked at him in mock dismay.

"I'll leave that to Mark," said Jason. "Where is he?"

"Somewhere." She glanced round vaguely. "Probably still trying to catch the big one."

They strolled towards the rest of the group, flopping down on well-used beach towels. Nicole ran a comb through her wet hair. It's almost as black as Tessa's, Jason noticed. She re-applied lavish amounts of sun tan cream to her arms and legs. "Want some?" She offered the tube to Jason.

"No thanks. I'm not staying long. Have to be back for the paper round. Have you seen David?"

"He was here earlier. He's probably gone bird watching." She rubbed the cream into her long tanned legs.

Jason was used to David wandering off on his own. They had been friends since early schooldays when they'd both been `*newies*' in the same class, desperate to fit in. David's father was American and his mother Xhosa. They had met at the University of California. The family had lived in America until David was ten-years-old when they had returned to his mother's home South Africa. Jason's parents had emigrated from the north of England to Durban when he was the same age. The two boys had formed a bond when the other children made fun of their accents. Mark had been the main instigator of the teasing - until Jason had threatened to give him a going over, and they'd ended up slugging it out. Although Mark had been the bigger of the two boys Jason was more agile and the fight ended when a teacher separated them and made the boys shake hands. The three of them had been friends ever since.

Jason glanced up the beach to the conservation area a few hundred metres away, which was a popular bird-watching spot. But there was no sign of David.

He turned his attention to the surfers. A powerful wave was building up. It feathered, and as it started to curl, one of the riders pushed his board into the wall of water. In one fluid movement he was standing and angled into the wave. He sped along the face of water until he ended up on the shoulder where he swung the board and cutback into the pocket. Pumping the board to maintain his speed, he manoeuvred through the breaking sections of the wave, swinging the board to hit the lip and then dropping back.

Jason watched him ride the thundering sheet of water until it began to lose its power. When he kicked off, Jason recognised Mark. A shallower wave carried him to the shore. He grabbed his board and jogged up the beach.

"How's it?" He shook his spiky wet hair over Jason, who sprang out of the way of the cold droplets. "Want to borrow my board?"

"No thanks. I have to do my round."

"Oh, that's right, paper time. D'you think you'll see Tessa? I've kept the cellphone with me in case she tried calling, but I haven't heard anything."

"Who's Tessa?" demanded Nicole, with a hint of suspicion.

"Nothing to do with you." Mark squeezed his still wet hair over her.

She squealed, flicking him with a towel. "Get off, brush-head."

Jason was used to their squabbling and he didn't let it bother him. "I'm not giving up on Tessa. I'm going to see if there is a way in to 69. If there is, I'll go back later, when it's dark."

Mark was thoughtful as he dried himself with a towel. "You're really determined, aren't you?"

"I guess I am," said Jason.

"Let me know if you need any help," said Mark, flopping down on the towel.

"I'll get you on the cellphone if I need you. Don't forget about tomorrow night. Caitlin's counting on you." Jason jumped up and dusted the sand off his legs. "And wear decent shoes."

Mark pulled a face. "If I don't hear from you tonight, I'll see you tomorrow."

Jason sprinted across the sand and mounted his bike. With a roar, he sped off to collect his papers.

The bag was heavier on a Friday because of the weekend supplements. He hoisted it onto the bike and then read the note with the alterations or additions to his round. There were two holiday stops, one new customer, and one cancellation - 69 Ocean Drive. Damn. Perhaps they'd connected him to the phone call.

He checked his watch. He'd try to reach 69 Ocean Drive at his usual time. This was the only connection he had with Tessa. She might try some way of making contact. But he would have to be more careful now.

When he reached Ocean Drive, he realised the high brick wall was now topped by an electrified wire fence. A sign by the gate warned potential intruders to BEWARE. The house was a fortress. As far as he could see, his options for getting in were down to zero.

He stopped his bike on the grass verge outside the house and killed the motor. The boundary wall was high enough so he wasn't visible from the upstairs rooms, but it also meant he couldn't see them from where he stood. There was a large Hibiscus overhanging the wall on the opposite side of the road and he crossed and stood in its shadow. He still wouldn't be visible to anyone glancing out of the window. He would only show himself if Tessa appeared.

He waited for five minutes before he saw a shadowy figure move across one of the windows. But it didn't re-appear, and no one looked out or tried to make any kind of signal. He waited a further ten minutes before giving up to finish his round.

There had to be some way of getting in touch with Tessa. Letters were out, and so were telephones. And it would take the most sophisticated of burglars to get through the new security.

He was still thinking about the problem that evening while he and his father fitted the inflatable floats on the chopper. They had taken it into the garden and set it on the lawn. Jason fuelled it and held the rotor steady while his father started the motor. It burst into life and Jason adjusted the throttle by gently easing back the stick on the radio transmitter.

"Keep the revs down," his father instructed.

Jason sighed. He knew not to cause the chopper to lift. It was almost a metre in length, and the garden with its abundance of trees, was too confined for a maiden flight. Tonight they were checking that the motor was running smoothly ready for its inaugural flight in the morning.

"Seems to be behaving." His father was listening to the steady pitch of the motor as Jason worked the throttle.

Satisfied that everything was behaving as it should, they were returning the chopper to the workshop when Caitlin called to Jason. "Mark's on the phone. He and David are at the club. They want to know if you're going down."

He's probably wondering about 69, thought Jason. "Tell him, no thanks. I'll see him tomorrow," Jason yelled back.

Mr Hunter peered over his glasses. "Has he got another new cellphone?"

"I expect so," said Jason. "His Dad's firm picks up part of the bill."

"It doesn't seem that long ago that people were using carrier pigeons," said Mr Hunter, adjusting the silencer. "And now look where we are."

Jason had a vision of himself and Mark using pigeon post. No doubt Nicole's two cats would cause a few communication problems. He was chuckling to himself when he had another thought. If carrier pigeons could carry messages, so could model helicopters. The seed of an idea began to take shape. It wouldn't be easy. Flying the chopper close to a building by itself was a tricky manoeuvre. However, it was the only plan that made any sense.

He was thinking through the possibilities as he watched his father, who, with infinite patience, was re-tightening already tight screws. Weeks of labour had gone into building the chopper. Jason imagined his father's reaction to a request to use it to pass a message to a mysterious girl who was possibly being held captive at 69 Ocean Drive. In his mind's eye he saw his father peering solemnly over the rim of his glasses, frowning, and with a sigh saying, "Is this another of your fanciful imaginings?"

There didn't seem any way he could convince his father that Tessa really did need help. And if he found out that they'd already been to the police, who'd explained that nothing could be done, then there was no way that he would condone them interfering. His heart sinking, Jason concluded that he would have to use the chopper without his father's permission.

However, that wasn't the only problem with his plan. The most pressing one was to learn how to fly the Jet Ranger. And to learn quickly. "I'll put the radio on charge," he said. "So we can make an early start tomorrow."

Saturday morning was usually a relaxed breakfast for the Hunter family. There was time to talk, and for Mr Hunter to catch up on the week's events and discover what his family had been up to. But when Jason sat down at the table he saw that Caitlin had already left.

"She wanted to get to the fresh-produce market early. For that 25th she's doing tonight." Jason's mother passed him the cereal box. "It's an important job. A big sugar baron. She's hoping it will be an opening to more work. You never know who will be there."

"Probably a lot of old wrinklies," muttered Jason.

"Hey," said Mr Hunter. "Your mother and I haven't had our 25th yet."

"Case proven," said Jason, grinning. He ducked as his father plucked a lychee from the fruit bowl and tossed it at him.

"I hope you're going to pick that up." Mrs Hunter frowned as the lychee missed its target and rolled under the dresser.

Jason glanced at his father, who shrugged. "I'm such an old wrinkly. I'll leave it to you youngsters to climb under furniture."

Jason retrieved the lychee and pitched it to his father who, taken by surprise, fumbled the catch. "I hope your reactions are going to be sharper with the chopper," quipped Jason.

"It's time you two went," said Mrs Hunter, hiding a smile as she clattered the dishes into a pile and carried them through to the kitchen.

"Come on, Dad," said Jason. He was eager to get the chopper into the air. It would take quite a few hours' practice before he would feel confident enough to fly it over the wall of 69.

The school playing fields were usually deserted. They had learned that bystanders of the "How's this work" and "What's this for?" brigade had a tendency to fiddle, which could prove disastrous if it went unnoticed.

Jason carried the chopper to the middle of the soccer field while his father followed with the radio transmitter, fuel, and a box of miniature tools for making minor adjustments.

Nothing had been damaged in transit and the radio was operating properly so Jason started the motor.

Mr Hunter kept the rotors disengaged until Jason was clear. In some cases the tip speed of the rotor blades could reach 400 k.p.h. As the blades and tail rotor began to spin Mr Hunter gently eased the throttle forward, lifting the chopper a few centimetres off the ground. The gyro automatically adjusted the tail rotor to keep the chopper straight. It skidded along the ground on the inflatable training gear while Mr Hunter felt the throttle response of the engine. If the chopper started to tip, the rotor blades would hit the ground and smash.

Jason could see the tension in his father's face. Flying a chopper was like trying to balance on top of a beach ball. It was a case of constantly responding to what was happening. "How does it feel?" asked Jason. "It looks as if there's a bit of vibration."

Mr Hunter set the chopper down. "The tail seems to be shaking. The main blades could be out of balance."

Jason corrected it with a rubber band over one of the blades. "I'd better check that nothing's been shaken loose." Not only could loose components cause more vibration, they could also cause electrical interference. Jason knew he had to be patient while they made these minor, but vital adjustments, but he was aching to get the chopper airborne. He needed it to get a letter to Tessa.

Then he thought ahead. How would she reply? Could he hover for long enough? Would someone hear it? There were still plenty of problems to be solved.

4

Satisfied that the blades were balanced, and the chopper was now hovering as it should, Jason's father gradually swung the tail round until he could point the chopper in any direction and hold it there. "Gyro seems to be working okay," he said.

Jason breathed a sigh of relief. Perhaps now they could start hovering off the ground. "Let's re-fuel before we try any manoeuvres." He hoped his father would also relinquish the transmitter box.

By lunchtime the Jet Ranger was responding smoothly. "I think that's enough for today." Mr Hunter switched off the chopper and the radio.

They packed up their equipment, and back in the workshop did a proper job of balancing the rotor blades. Jason reckoned that with a few more hours' practise he would be proficient enough for the more complicated manoeuvres.

Mark arrived at six o'clock. His waiter's white shirt and black trousers were carefully folded in his backpack. "Where is this party of Cait's?" He dumped his bag on the kitchen table.

"She's given me a map. Shouldn't be hard to find. It's a big place on one of the sugar estates." Jason pulled the paper out of his pocket.

They studied the scrawled instructions Caitlin had left. "I think I know where it is," said Mark. "You follow me."

"Okay. But I'll keep the map. Just in case."

"Would I get you lost?"

"Quite likely. That's not the point. Look, there's something I want you to think about on the way."

"What?" asked Mark suspiciously.

"I've got a plan for contacting Tessa. But there're a few problems."

Mark sighed. "I might have known. What's the plan?"

"I'm going to use the chopper - fly it over the wall with a letter attached."

Mark let out a low whistle. "Come on, d'you think your Dad's going to let you risk an expensive piece of equipment like the Jet Ranger?"

"I'm not going to tell him."

There was a dubious look on Mark's face. "It's your funeral if you smash it. But could you really fly it well enough?"

"With a bit more practise. But there might be a problem getting Tessa's reply. And we'll have to make sure she's alone."

“Why not give her a cellphone?” Mark suggested.

“That’s an idea. But who has a spare one? Let's think about it on the way." Jason shrugged on his leather jacket.

Within half an hour they were turning off the highway and onto a dirt road bordered by fields of tall sugar cane that seemed to stretch forever. As they tipped the crest of a hill the house was suddenly before them, a stately landmark in a sea of waving green. Drawing nearer, Jason saw that the gates were open. A wide gravel driveway snaked round the house. On each side lay spacious crew-cut lawns edged with pink and white busy lizzie, pale blue petunia and orange marigolds and nasturtium.

They slowed as they approached the gate. A uniformed security guard stepped out from behind the gatepost and signalled them to stop.

"We're probably not the kind of visitors he's expecting." Jason grinned at Mark.

The boys explained their mission. Before they were allowed in, the doubtful guard spoke into a two-way radio to confirm their story.

"That's it," Jason exclaimed.

"What is?"

"A two-way radio. That's what we need to talk to Tessa. That way we could all keep in touch." He looked eagerly at Mark. "Your Dad’s into electronics.

What are the chances of you getting hold of some two-way radios?"

"If I scratched round I could probably come up with something. But how are you going to get a radio to her?"

"Fly it in on the chopper of course." Jason almost gave a whoop as the guard waved them through.

Jason's mind was whirling with plans for the two-way radios as they rode round to the rear of the house. The familiar white van with `Caitlin's Catering' emblazoned on the side was standing beside one of the four garages adjoining the house. They parked their scramblers next to the van and went in through the kitchen door. Caitlin was in her usual pre-dinner fluster. Her wavy brown hair was tied back with a neat red velvet band, but a few wisps had escaped onto her face. She brushed them away with the back of her hand. When she saw the boys, she gave a sigh of relief, checking her watch as they sauntered in.

"We're not late, Caty dear," Mark said sweetly before she could say anything.

"Hurry up and get changed. I want you to check the table settings first." She was arranging lettuce leaves on plates.

Jason flashed a grin at Mark. "Excuse my sister's rudeness. She does usually say hello. It must be the stress."

"Sorry Jase. I'm running late."

The family cook, who'd been requisitioned to assist, left her job of turning the salmon mousse out of their moulds and onto the lettuce leaves, to show the boys to the downstairs cloakroom where they could change.

"Are you serious about those radios?" asked Mark, drawing his T-shirt over his head.

"Can you think of a better plan?" Jason glanced in the mirror as he combed the flopping locks of hair out of his eyes. "The radios would solve all our communication problems. The security companies all use them."

"But would you be able to fly the chopper with a radio dangling underneath? Wouldn't it make it unsteady?"

"The Jet Ranger would have the power. But I'd need some practise to get the balance right. Will you see what you can do?"

"I'll have a look when I go into Dad's office on Monday," said Mark, wincing as he buttoned the tight collar of his shirt.

Returning to the kitchen they had to submit to Caitlin's inspection and re-adjustment of their bow ties. However, when the spotlight of her attention focused on Mark's feet she let out a gasp, "What are you wearing!"

He glanced down and wiggled his toes. "Beach thongs. You said I should wear something comfortable."

Caitlin turned a horrified face to Jason. "Black shoes. I told you to tell him black shoes!"

Mark held a foot up for inspection. "They are black."

Caitlin looked so distraught that Jason relented. "It's okay Cait. He's got proper black shoes in his bag." He bit his lip to stop himself laughing.

Caitlin gave them both a murderous look. He could see wasn't in the mood for games. "We'll check the table settings," he said, steering Mark away from his furious sister.

Muttering terrible threats, Caitlin returned to wrapping the individual Beef Wellingtons in their pastry cases.

There were to be thirty people for dinner and the first course had been planned for eight o'clock. By seven-thirty most of the guests had arrived and were having pre-dinner drinks in the lounge.

The boys had helped garnish the salmon mousse with dill, and cut the pumpernickel bread into neat triangles so that at five minutes to eight the first course was waiting on the table.

They were standing attentively, one each end of the table.

"Don't forget, serve from the right," instructed Caitlin, before hurrying back to the kitchen as the guests began filing in.

Mark grinned approvingly as two teenage girls appeared. They glanced coyly at Jason's lean chiselled face and Mark's tall muscular frame, giggling and exchanging looks as Jason pulled out their chairs. Obviously nieces of the host, he thought as they addressed the middle-aged man who was ushering everyone in, as Uncle John.

The rest of the guests were middle-aged or elderly. One distinguished looking man with a commanding voice sounded very English.

As instructed by Caitlin, Jason listened for comments on the meal. There were murmurs of approval for the mousse, except for one apologetic lady who was allergic to salmon.

When the first course had been cleared, Mark brought in the plates of Beef Wellington. Caitlin had poured a small portion of gravy on each of the plates, placed the wrapped beef on top, and decorated it with a sprig of fennel. Jason followed with the dish of vegetables. He felt quite proud of his sister's culinary skills. There were tender baby carrots, tiny new potatoes shiny with butter, and broccoli and cauliflower with melted cheese. The tempting smells were making him hungry. He hoped Caitlin had made a few extra portions.

"This looks delicious," exclaimed the allergic lady, piercing the juicy beef.

She's probably trying to make up for not eating the first course thought Jason as he spooned carrots onto her plate. Then the commanding English voice sitting next to her was saying, "They'll have to have some sort of reception. It's expected. Every new embassy does it." Jason's attention was at once riveted on the conversation. Could it be Tessa's embassy? Surely there couldn't be that many new ones.

"But where will they hold it?" The allergy lady speared a potato before turning to her companion. "They can't have it at those poky old offices they're using at the moment."

Jason should have been serving the next guest, but he tried stalling. "Would you care for more vegetables, sir?" The answer was a polite shake of the head. He was forced to move on, but his ear was still tuned to the conversation.

"Probably have it at the official residence," the man surmised. "I believe it's somewhere on Ocean Drive."

Jason nearly dropped the vegetable dish.

"Well I hope they don't serve any of that dreadful foreign food." The woman threw back her head and permitted herself a moment's laughter.

The vegetable dish was empty. Jason moved swiftly back to the kitchen. These people knew about the embassy. It was protocol to have a reception. If they went ahead with it, they would need caterers. His mind flooded with the possibilities.

Caitlin was placing the last of the Beef Wellingtons on their plates. "Caitlin," urged Jason. "You've got to impress these people."

She turned a harassed perspiring face to him. "Jason, what d'you think I'm trying to do - poison them?" She took the vegetable dish from him and ladled carrots into it.

Mark breezed in to collect the last of the Beef Wellingtons. He winked at Jason. "They fancy me."

"Who do?" demanded Caitlin.

"Two of the guests," said Mark mysteriously.

"Mark, if you mess this up..." threatened Caitlin.

He gave her one of his impish grins. Swooping up the plates, he turned to go. Jason was right behind him. "Listen Mark, be on your best behaviour. We have to make a good impression tonight."

"Why? What's so special about tonight?"

"I can't explain now. Just don't mess up," said Jason.

"You're seriously interfering with my love life. D'you know that?"

"You'll recover." Jason shoved him through the door.

He was hoping that the embassy would still be the subject of conversation, but the guests were now discussing horseracing and politics. When they started on the Pavlova the conversation had moved on to business investments. If only he could talk to the man in private - ask him what he knew about the embassy. However, the likelihood of that happening seemed pretty remote.

He poured the thick farm cream over the kiwi fruit and strawberries that Caitlin had piled on the Pavlova, and his mouth began to water. They had been so busy he hadn't even had time for a spoonful of carrots. He was starving. He wouldn't offer the guests seconds. He wasn't going to miss out on the Pavlova.

They served the cheese and biscuits on a wooden platter, and then Jason returned to the kitchen hoping there would be time to snatch something to eat, but the kitchen was steeped in the aroma of freshly percolated coffee. Caitlin was placing thin almond biscuits on each cup and saucer. "What d'you think, Jase?" She gave him an eager, expectant look, calm now that everything was almost over. "Did they like the food?"

"They seemed to," said Jason. "It looked good, and they ate everything. But I can't comment on the taste - yet." He threw her a meaningful look.

"It's okay, I've saved you some." She smiled and nodded towards a heaped plate standing on the counter.

"That's good," said Mark, slicing a piece of Beef Wellington and dropping into a chair. He stuffed a chunk of pastry into his mouth as the door opened and the hostess swept in, flushed with success, and a little too much wine.

"Caitlin, darling. What a divine meal."

Mark leapt to his feet, spluttered, and sprayed a blizzard of pastry crumbs over the floor.

"Are you all right, young man?"

Mark nodded, trying desperately not to choke.

Satisfied that she wouldn't have to summon medical assistance, she turned her attention back to Caitlin. "Come along, my dear." She ushered Caitlin to the door. "My guests would like to meet the chef."

Caitlin looked both pleased and panic-stricken as she whipped off her apron and thrust it at Jason. He gave her a thumbs-up.

The boys heard muffled laughter coming from the dining room, and then applause.

The kitchen door flew open and Caitlin appeared, beaming wildly, her cheeks aflame.

"Do they all know your name? Did you give everyone a business card?" Jason hovered anxiously as she re-tied her apron.

"Yes to the first, no to the second." She was still beaming. "Why are you so concerned?"

He lifted his shoulders and tried to sound casual. "I overheard someone saying something about a new South American embassy. Apparently new embassies hold receptions. If you got the job, it could bring you in a lot of work. Thought you might be interested."

"Maybe I'll ask around. Now come on, don't forget the coffee." She returned to the job in hand, depositing biscuits on the saucers.

Jason picked up the tray of cups while Mark carried the coffee-pot. "What was all that about?" he said, opening the door for Jason.

"Think about it," said Jason. "If Caitlin got the catering job at the embassy, we could get in as waiters."

"What some people won't do for love," sighed Mark.

5

"How did the dinner party go last night?" Mrs Hunter beamed, handing Jason the jam as the family enjoyed a leisurely Sunday breakfast.

Caitlin glanced at her brother. "Jason was impressed," she grinned. "He thinks I'm ready for the diplomatic corp."

"Eh?" Mr Hunter, his toast mid-way to his mouth, turned a surprised face to his son, whose interest in his sister's catering had never extended beyond a `what's left to eat?' or `how much are you going to pay me?'

"Some of the guests were discussing the new South American embassy." Jason ladled youngberry jam onto his toast and spread it carefully into the corners. "Apparently it's usual to have a reception. I thought it would be good business for Caitlin. You know, getting in with people who have expense-account functions."

"That sounds a good idea," agreed Mrs Hunter. "But how will they find out about Caitlin's Catering?"

Jason had already planned to drop one of Caitlin's cards in the post box at number 69. But that would be his little secret.

"I've got some contacts," said Caitlin. "I'll put some feelers out."

"Before you get too proud to cook for the likes of us, how about making some more toast," said Mr Hunter, handing Caitlin his empty plate. She grinned, still in the after-glow of the successful dinner party, and went through to the kitchen to cut more bread.

Sunday was Jason and his father's turn to do the breakfast dishes. After they had clattered about in the kitchen and put the plates back in all the wrong places so that Mrs Hunter would have to search them out, Mr Hunter announced, "We'll take the chopper down to the flying club."

Jason knew his father wanted to show it off. That was okay. It would give him the chance to ask the other members what they knew about flying close to buildings. Not that he was going to let them know why.

The flying field was in an odd-shaped corner of a cane field, about half the size of a soccer pitch. The members had grassed it and made a small tarred runway. There was a two-metre-high tower where a windsock fluttered languidly in the mild breeze as Jason and his father bumped along the dirt track.

They parked in the roped-off area reserved for spectators, and began unloading the station-wagon. Two men in faded T-shirts and shorts spotted with oil and fuel drips came over to admire the Jet Ranger. Jason stood patiently by as his father explained the intricacies of the building process.

They were fortunate there was only one other flier using the same radio frequency and they were able to get in a good hour's flying.

Jason avoided any fancy aerobatics so as not to risk damaging the chopper. He concentrated on mastering the controls. He would need quick reactions and good throttle response to handle the turbulence he'd been told to expect near buildings. It would be a risky manoeuvre hovering over the balcony at 69. He had better get another look at the layout of the area, find out how close the nearest trees were. Perhaps he could even draw a plan and work out possible crosswinds.

After lunch Jason rode down to the beach where he'd arranged to meet the boys for volleyball. But he couldn't concentrate on the game. Twice he touched the net, and he missed a couple of easy passes.

"Can't take late nights, eh, Jase?" Mark punched him on the arm.

"I've got other things on my mind," said Jason.

"Let's take a break." David tossed the ball to one of the onlookers and the boys collapsed onto their towels.

Mark pulled some Cokes out of his cooler bag. "So what's up now?" he said, handing out the ice-cold drinks.

"We need to work out the details of how we're going to get the radio to Tessa," said Jason.

"What radio?" asked David.

"Mark's going to get us two-way radios," explained Jason, slurping the fizzing liquid from the rim of the can. "I'm going to use the chopper to get one of them to her."

"Won't that be tricky? Can you fly that well?" said David, looking ahead for possible problems.

"I'll get in some practice flying near the school buildings. But I'll need a closer look at that balcony," said Jason.

"What about the noise from the chopper's engine? Won't it attract the crow?" David wanted to know.

"I was counting on you and Mark to distract her," said Jason.

"How are we going to do that?" asked David, not wanting to leave anything to chance.

"I'm sure Mark will come up with something." Jason made a face at his friend. "He doesn't usually have difficulty getting into trouble."

Mark was ready with a retort, but David was asking, "And how do you know when Tessa will be on the balcony?"

"I don't know," admitted Jason.

David gulped down his Coke, his brow creased in thought. "We could leave a message in the sand, but we'd risk the crow seeing it."

"Tessa probably does her studying on the balcony. I'll just have to hang about until I see her," said Jason.

Mark got to his feet and drained the last of his Coke. "Come on. If we're going to reconnoitre, let's get on with it. Tessa could be there now."

Snatching up their gear, they threw it into their backpacks and shouted a "See, ya," to the rest of the gang before heading for their scramblers.

As they approached the rear of number 69 there was no sign of life on the balcony. But there were Sunday afternoon shrieks and yells and splashing sounds coming from the swimming pools of neighbouring properties.

"I've got a pencil and paper here somewhere to draw a rough plan," said Jason, rifling through his bag.

"You'd get a better view from one of those trees." Mark pointed to the neighbouring garden that had a number of trees growing close to the fence. "We'd be able to see the whole garden. Might even see Tessa." He started for the tree.

"You're right." Jason was right behind him.

"Wait a minute," cautioned David. "Have you thought this through?"

Mark sighed. Now that he was involved in the plan, he wanted to get on with it. "What's wrong now?"

"You're going to look pretty conspicuous in that tree. Not to mention suspicious."

He was right, Jason realised. "What do you suggest?"

David was already pulling his white T-shirt over his head. His shorts were dark green. He threw out his arms. "Who's going to see me?"

Jason and Mark looked at David's coffee-coloured skin and then at each other and shrugged. "He's right. Perfect camouflage."

Taking Jason's pencil and paper David said, "I'm better at technical drawing than you. And I've got my binoculars." He slung them round his neck, tucked the carefully folded paper in the waistband of his shorts, and pushed the pencil into the tight curls on his head.

Instead of choosing the tree closest to the fence of 69, he selected the next one, which had thicker foliage.

The lowest branch was well over two metres from the ground, but with a volleyball spring he leapt up and easily grasped the overhanging limb. In a neat gymnastic move, he had swung himself into the tree.

"What can you see?" Jason kept his voice low.

David glanced into the garden in which the tree stood. About fifty metres away a young couple and two toddlers were splashing in a kidney-shaped swimming pool. Beside it was a thatched umbrella where an elderly couple was sipping tea. They gave no indication that they had seen him.

He turned his attention to number 69. Rockeries spilling pink and white impatiens bordered a sweeping lawn. Water trickled down an outcrop of natural rock into a free-form swimming pool made to look like a mountain pool. Three white plastic pool chairs with bright yellow cushions stood under the shade of a leafy Jacaranda tree. David noticed three empty glasses and a towel on a table next to the chairs.

"Can you see Tessa?" Jason was getting impatient.

"Not yet." David adjusted the binoculars and focused on the buildings. Separate from the house was a change room cum bar with sliding glass doors. One door was slightly open, but there didn't appear to be anyone inside.

He trained the binoculars on the house. A tiled veranda ran the length of the house. At the end closest to him, David could see a walled yard, which he assumed, led off the kitchen. Next to it was what appeared to be a small breakfast room. At the far end French windows opened into the formal lounge.

"Come on, Dave. What's going on?" urged Mark.

"I can't see anyone at the moment. But there must be someone around because the doors are all open."

"Get the drawing done while you've got the chance," said Jason.

David hooked his leg over the branch and leaned on the trunk to steady himself while he sketched.

"Plot the position of all the trees," said Jason.

David had almost completed the drawing when he saw figures moving in the breakfast room. A tall, slim, balding man with a deep tan appeared on the veranda. He was wearing red swimming shorts and a towel was draped around his neck. He headed for the change room, slid open the doors, and went inside.

David focused the binoculars, watching the man as he slipped behind the bar and poured himself a drink. He dropped a couple of ice-cubes in the glass and carried it out to the chair under the tree.

Jason was getting edgy. "What's up? What are you looking at?"

"There's a man in the garden," David called in a low voice.

"What's he look like?"

David described him. "A smooth-looking guy who's going bald,"

"Doesn't sound like the pirate. He's got a moustache and looks more like a wrestler," said Jason.

"Shush. Someone else is coming out."

A woman in a flowered beach robe appeared, followed by a young girl in a black bikini. It had to be the crow and Tessa. The crow headed for the shady tree and joined the balding man at the table. With long leisurely strides Tessa made for the swimming pool. She was certainly a looker, David decided, admiring her lithe athletic figure. With hardly a splash she made a perfect dive into the pool and struck out for the shallow end.

"Who is it?" demanded Jason.

"The crow and Tessa."

"Tessa! What's she doing?"

David watched Tessa climb out of the pool and walk across to the couple sitting at the table. She picked up the towel and dried herself before sitting down. "They're sitting at the table. It looks like he's offering to get her a drink. Wait a minute. He's put his hand on her arm."

"What's Tessa doing?" said Jason, alarmed.

"She's pulled away. She looks annoyed. He seems to be trying to calm her."

This was too much for Jason. "I'm coming up to have a look." He swung into the tree.

"I'm with you," said Mark.

"Don't. Stay where you are," hissed David. "I don't think this branch is strong enough for all of us."

But Jason had scrambled up to sit beside David, his thoughts centred on Tessa's safety.

"You clowns!" said David, as Mark heaved himself onto the branch.

"Let me have the binoculars," said Jason. "I want to see if Tessa's in any danger." He was busy focusing them when there was a slight cracking sound.

"Look out!" yelled Mark as a louder craaack came from the branch as it began splintering from the tree.

David, who was close to the trunk, grabbed frantically at the nearest branch and held on. Jason and Mark weren't so lucky. As the branch sheared off they were thrown forward, hitting the wall with a force that winded them. The smaller branches whip-lashed and Jason tasted blood as one caught him on the lip.

Mark's shirt tore and he felt a burning pain as the concrete wall gashed his arm.

David watched helplessly as the branch crashed to the ground, carrying the boys with it. He heard a shout. The balding man was yelling, "Raul," and the crow was staring in their direction. She grabbed Tessa's arm and dragged her towards the house.

A heavy-set man with a dark moustache appeared from the kitchen area. The balding man yelled unintelligible instructions at him. To David's horror he saw both men sprinting towards the gate.

"Jason, Mark. Get out. Run! They're coming through the gate."

Mark was still winded, and the branch was across his legs, pinning him down. Jason, his head spinning with the shock of the fall, scrambled to his feet. He started to drag the heavy limb off Mark.

David swung along the branch and dropped onto the soft sand. As he landed, he heard the sharp sound of the bolt being thrown on the gate. "Come on," he urged, grappling with the branch. They heaved it off Mark's legs just before the gate burst open.

Mark felt a hand grasp his shirt collar and he was hauled to his feet.

6

"Get out. Run, Jase!" gasped Mark as Raul spun him round so that their noses were almost touching. There was a murderous expression on the man's face as he spat out, "I'll teach you kids to spy." He lashed out and the back of his hand connected with Mark's ear, sending a flash of pain shooting through his skull.

Jason and David weren't about to leave Mark to the mercy of Raul. Jason flung himself across the sand in a crashing tackle that brought the man down. The shock was enough to make him loosen his grip, and Mark darted away.

But the balding man grasped Jason's hair in a painful hold and hauled him to his feet, dragging him towards the gate. Jason knew that once he was inside, technically he would be on foreign soil and anything could happen.

David waded in. In a volleyball stance he brought his fists up and caught the man under the elbow. There was a crack and the man yelled in pain and released his grip on Jason.

Now Raul was on his feet and raging. His right fist shot forward to connect with David's jaw, but David saw it coming and twisted slightly so that the fist glanced along his cheek. But the impact was enough to knock him to the ground. The next instant Raul's foot was slicing through the air towards his head. Mark was ready and kicked the man behind his knee, sending him sprawling.

The balding man lashed out at Jason with a powerful left jab. Jason ducked skilfully and the man's fist carved through the air. Off-balance, he thudded into the sand.

With both of the men down, Jason saw their chance to escape. "Let's go," he yelled.

But Raul was not going to be outwitted by three boys. He hurled himself at David in a flying tackle. When David saw a hundred kilograms of fury rocketing towards him, he threw himself to one side. But the man had weight and size on his side and he grabbed David's wrist in a crushing grip.

David fought furiously to free himself. Thanks to Nicole's sun cream, his arm was slippery. He freed his wrist with a neat twist. At the same time he swung his knee up and planted it in the man's stomach and he groaned, doubled over, and sank to his knees.

"Run, Dave," yelled Mark.

David waited long enough to snatch up his binoculars and T-shirt and then sprinted across the sand after Mark and Jason.

The boys didn't stop until they reached their bikes. When they glanced back there was no sign of the men following them.

"Phew," said Mark in a quiet voice, running his fingers through his hair.

"That was close," whispered Jason.

They looked at each other wide-eyed with shock. Then with sudden relief the three of them burst out laughing.

"Come on," said Jason. "Let's go back to my place and discuss what we're going to do next."

Back in Jason's bedroom he put on a Stones tape that Caitlin had made from her mother's collection of old records.

"Hey, these aren't bad," said David. "Could you make me a copy?"

"Sure." Jason dabbed antiseptic on his cut lip.

Mark inspected his ripped shirt. There were grazes down his arm, and a bruise was forming on his shoulder. "Hey, Jase, lend me a T-shirt. I don't want to have to explain this."

"They're in the top drawer." He nodded towards the wardrobe. "But don't take the rhino one." Seeing Striker, the family tabby curled on the jumble of shoes at the bottom of the cupboard, he warned, "And watch out for the cat."

Mark kept his eye on the family pet, knowing his sometimes painful inclination to claw the legs of unsuspecting victims. Mark found a SPCA shirt emblazoned with a grinning cat. It had the legend `Tabby or not Tabby' under the picture. He grinned and pulled it over his head.

Jason offered the antiseptic to the others. David was careful to wash the graze on his cheek before treating it with the antiseptic.

Mark poured the remainder of the liquid on his arm, from where it dribbled pinkly and unnoticed onto the bedcover.

"Dave, what happened to the sketch?" asked Jason.

David pulled the crumpled paper from his shorts and Jason pushed aside some notebooks and pencils and spread the paper across his desk. He chewed his lip thoughtfully as he pored over the sketch drawn in David's precise hand.

Mark lay on the bed thumbing through Jason's ancient Mad magazines.

"That looks pretty straightforward," said Jason, mentally calculating the distances. "The chopper should be able to clear that tree easily. If Tessa's at the table in the middle of the balcony it should be out of the way of any crosswinds from the corners of the house." He put the paper to one side. "What other useful info did we get?"

"Your so-called pirate has a damn heavy fist," said Mark, rubbing the side of his head. "I think I'm getting a cauliflower ear."

"It'll match your potato head." Jason dodged the pillow that Mark hurled at him, wincing as the sudden movement hurt his bruised chest.

"The pirate's name is Raul." David shoved Mark's legs aside to sit on the bed. "And he obviously works for baldy."

"But who is baldy? And more importantly - what is his relationship to Tessa?" said Jason seriously.

"And to the crow," added David.

"He could be the embassy head," suggested Jason.

"I should think he'd have to be the head, otherwise how could he keep Tessa against her will?" David was quick to analyse. "Everyone living in the house would have to know what's going on."

"We'll have to wait for Tessa to give us the answers," said Mark.

"Are you sure you can get some two-way radios?" Jason swung his leg over the chair and propped his arms on the backrest.

"Most of the big firms have security patrols that use them. There are usually several in for repair, or for up-grading. I expect there'll be a few older models lying around. It'll be a case of tuning them into a spare channel."

"We'll need three radios." Jason counted them off on his fingers. "One for Tessa, one for me, and one for you two to communicate with me while you're distracting the crow and her buddies."

"We still haven't worked out how we're going to do the distracting," mused David, eyes narrowed in thought.

"Maybe there'll be some trees in the front garden we can fall out of," said Mark, grinning.

Jason hurled the pillow back at him. "Very funny."

"It's going to be more difficult now that they can recognise us." David's mind was working ahead.

"Not if we keep our helmets on," Mark pointed out.

"Mark's right," agreed Jason. "With your visors down no one will recognise you."

"We'll have to get the crow and the others as far as the gate, otherwise they could still hear the chopper," said David.

"How about telling them we've got a delivery for them?" Mark looked at Jason, who frowned, "They might open the gate and expect you to deliver it to the door."

"And even if they decided to fetch it themselves, it would only take one of them." David was already ahead of them. "We'll have to cause enough of a commotion to make all the staff leave the house."

"Let's fake an accident." Jason was fired with the idea. "Make out that Mark's bike is wedged under the gate. David can call them on the intercom and talk in garbled Xhosa so they can't ask too many details.

That should bring them out." He looked earnestly at David. "You can speak Xhosa?"

David let out a breath. "Sort of...There wasn't much use for Xhosa in the States."

"Good. We'll sort out the finer points of the plan later."

There was a knock on the door and Jason's mother called to ask if the boys were staying for a Sunday pizza supper. They didn't need any persuasion and soon all three were hurtling down the stairs to the kitchen.

The next morning Jason persuaded Caitlin to drive him and the chopper down to the playing fields so he could get in some flying practise.

There was a slight breeze, similar to the one that came off the sea at Ocean Drive. He carried the chopper to the centre of the field and made the usual pre-flight checks. Flying it below shoulder height he was able to watch its responses.

Gradually he moved closer to the buildings. When he was within a few metres of the classrooms the chopper suddenly dipped. It had hit a pocket of turbulence. Jason instinctively corrected the settings, bringing it back on course. However, the manoeuvre had taken the whirling blades dangerously close to the brick walls. The unstable air buffeted the small craft. It took all Jason's concentration to keep it steady. Gradually he brought the tail round until he could direct it away from the classrooms. Tense with concentration he brought the chopper down.

When it settled on the field, he let out a relieved breath. Satisfied with the model's handling, and moderately pleased with his own performance, he packed up and set off on the long walk home.

There was a message waiting for him. *`Phone Mark at his Dad's office'* Caitlin had scrawled. It must be about the radios, thought Jason punching in the number.

Mark had discovered four radios in the back of a cupboard. The owner had left them for repair and never bothered to pick them up. "They're quite small. They'll easily fit into your hand," explained Mark.

"That's great. How much d'you reckon they'll weigh?"

"About 350 - 400 gms," Mark estimated.

"The Ranger should manage to lift that easily. Is there any problem with us borrowing them?"

"Not as long as we don't do any damage. The owner might still claim them."

"Bring them round tonight. I'll attach one to the chopper and get in some practise flying with it tomorrow."

So far, so good, thought Jason as he wiped down the Jet Ranger and returned it to the workshop.

He threw some polony and pickle onto a sandwich and finished off the remaining sausage rolls

Caitlin had left, before riding down to Ocean Drive in the hope of seeing Tessa.

The beach was deserted, except for a couple of fishermen trying their luck in the breaking waves. The sun glinted on the sea, and far out he could see a few ships at anchor, evidently waiting for a berth in the harbour.

He found a place in the dunes behind number 69 where he could watch the balcony and be hidden from view if anyone should glance in his direction.

Rummaging in his backpack he found his baseball cap and pulled it over his eyes. He brought out the sketch David had made, and a pencil for making notes. There was also packed a Frederick Forsyth novel and a model aeroplane magazine to pass the time. It would be three hours at the most, before his newspaper round.

From where he sat he could see the tops of the trees and the balcony, and he spent some time working out where the chopper should take off. While he was marking one of the dunes on the sketch he heard the splutter of a lawnmower. When it roared into life he realised it was in the garden of 69. It was a powerful motor, far noisier than the chopper. If only he could persuade the gardener to start it up while the chopper was airborne. But he didn't even know who was using the mower. It was too risky climbing into another tree, and besides, he didn't have any binoculars.

Settling back with his book, he glanced towards the balcony at frequent intervals in case Tessa made an appearance.

Although he was in partial shade the afternoon sun was uncomfortably hot and he was glad of the can of Coke he'd thrown into his bag. The liquid was luke-warm, but it was enough to quench his thirst.

After sitting reading for almost an hour his eyes began to close. On the point of splashing his face in the surf, he saw a figure on the balcony.

It was Tessa in shorts and a yellow halter-top and she was carrying some books. He cursed himself for not asking David for the binoculars. She settled at the table and spread the books as though she were studying.

What was going on in that house? If it were an embassy, what did they want with Tessa? Why would they hold her prisoner and yet still allow her to study?

He waited until he was sure she was alone before making himself visible. Pulling off his cap he waved it, willing her to look up. But she didn't respond.

The sound of the lawnmower had been replaced by the high-pitched whine of a lawn edger. She wouldn't hear if he whistled.

He waved again. He had to attract her attention before someone else spotted him.

Then something caught her attention. One of the fishermen was walking along the shoreline. Now was his chance. He waved again. At last, she had seen him. She glanced around before waving back.

He signalled her to stay where she was. Picking up a stout twig, he wrote in the sand. WEDNESDAY 3 P.M. SAME PLACE.

She gave him a thumbs-up.

He wanted to write more. To tell her not to worry. But he knew that every minute he lingered increased the chances of being seen. Wiping out the message with his foot, he was suddenly aware of the heavy wooden gate swinging open.

His jaw tightened as a man emerged through the gate. He was carrying a menacing looking machete.

7

Jason felt a cold trickle of perspiration run down his neck. He nerved himself, ready to run.

The man was wearing khaki trousers and a matching short-sleeved shirt. A straw Stetson was pulled low over his eyes. He seemed to be looking straight at Jason.

Cool it, Jason told himself. Destroy the message first. You can still out-run him if you're quick. Keeping his eye on the man, he scraped his foot through the sand. There was still a fair distance between the two of them. About to race off, he saw the man suddenly raise the machete. Was he going to hurl it? Jason's breath caught in his throat. He tried to figure the odds against outrunning a flying machete. Better wait and face it. At least he would see it coming and have an even chance of ducking.

But as quickly as he had raised it, the man brought the machete down, splintering the thorny bush growing close to the wall.

Jason's taut nerves relaxed and he let out a low breath. It was the gardener, evidently cutting the bush back.

Casually, Jason picked up his belongings. Tessa was still on the balcony, but he did not dare risk waving.

Back home, he went to Caitlin's room in search of her business cards. They were stacked in a neat pile on her dresser, glossy red, with gold embossed writing, designed and made by one of her college friends. He tucked one into his shirt pocket and quietly closed the door.

After he'd collected the newspapers he kept to his usual delivery time. However, when he reached Ocean Drive he was careful to keep the throttle of the bike low so as not to attract attention as he slipped Caitlin's card into the box at No 69.

Now he had to wait for Mark to bring the two-way radios.

Mark and David arrived shortly after supper and the boys took the radios to the workshop.

"I made contact with Tessa," said Jason explaining about the encounter. "I've told her three o'clock on Wednesday afternoon. I hope that's OK with you two."

"Fine by me." Mark was scanning the radio channels.

"I was going bird-watching. But I guess I can do that in the morning," agreed David.

Mark consulted the list of frequencies. "We'll have to set the radios on the same frequency." There were four hand-held FM transceivers with compact rubber aerials. He handed one each to Jason and David. "They work on 144 MHz."

They chose one of the lesser-used frequencies and Mark tuned in each radio.

"Are the batteries fully charged?" asked David.

"I put new ones in. Come on, let's see what the reception's like. Jason, you stay here. David and I will go into the garden."

Mark made for the front garden and David the back. Soon they heard the slightly crackly voice of Jason asking; "Can you hear me?"

"Yeh." Mark's voice was much clearer. "Turn the squelch button until there's no background hiss."

Then David's voice came over the air. "What's the range?"

"Probably between five and ten kilometres," replied Mark.

"D'you think we'd be able to hear Tessa from here?" Jason was hoping to be able to talk to her from the privacy of his bedroom.

"Maybe. Depends on the terrain."

"It's fairly flat. There aren't any big hills or anything."

"We'll only find out for sure on Wednesday," said Mark.

Jason summoned them back to the workshop. "I want to sort out how I'm going to hitch the radio to the chopper."

While he was studying the chopper's skids, David was still thinking about the communication. "I know there are only three of us, but we ought to have some sort of radio discipline. Like saying *`over'* when you've finished speaking. Or *`break'* if you have an emergency. It's better than everyone trying to talk at once."

Mark looked sceptical. But Jason agreed with David. "Might as well do it properly. We don't want any mistakes."

"O.K. Over and out," conceded Mark with a grin.

Each radio had a carrying strap. Jason hunted through the squirrel's nest of rubbish in the workshop until he unearthed a length of stout wire. He measured and cut it before bending it into a loop that would fit over the chopper's skids. He slipped the radio's strap into the loop. When he put the loop of wire over the skids the radio hung about half a metre below the chopper.

David looked dubious. "Are you sure it won't act as a pendulum and cause the chopper to swing?"

"It should be O.K. I'll try flying it tomorrow," said Jason. "But I'll need someone to help. I want to see how easy it is to slip the radio off the skids when the chopper's in the air."

"It's going to be tricky with those whirling blades."

"I'll keep the chopper high so you have to reach up."

"All right," David finally agreed. "We'll see you at the field tomorrow morning."

"Sorry, but I promised my Dad I'd help out at work," said Mark regretfully.

"Let's keep in touch with the radios," suggested Jason.

"Let's not. The less people who know we've got them, the better," said Mark, looking a little sheepish.

Jason wondered whether Mark's father knew he had borrowed the radios, but thought it better not to ask.

After breakfast the following morning Caitlin dropped Jason off at the playing field again. "Have you heard anything about that embassy job?" he ventured as the van pulled into the school grounds.

"Nothing definite. But I did hear that someone has been making enquiries at the college about catering firms." She looked at him quizzically. "Why are you so interested in this particular job?"

Jason shrugged. "No special reason. It's just that I could use the money if you need waiters."

"Got a new girlfriend?"

"Sort of."

She gave him a questioning smile as he lifted the chopper out of the van. He banged the door shut and waved as she roared off.

She'd hardly gone when David arrived. His father dropped him off on his way to lecture at the university.

David was swinging a crash helmet. "What's that for?"

"I'm not taking any chances with that chopper hovering over my head." He tapped the yellow and black dome as if to reassure himself of the calibre of its protection.

Jason slipped the radio over the chopper's skids, positioning it directly below the main shaft. It had to be between the blades to maintain the machine's centre of gravity.

David kept a safe distance while Jason started the motor. The machine slowly rose into the air. Jason could feel the slight drag of the load and increased the revs to compensate for the extra weight. He flew it in a wide circle to make sure the radio did not swing and cause problems with the controls. When he had it hovering steadily, he signalled to David to remove the radio.

With the helmet firmly in place, David reached up for the radio. As it slid forward over the skids Jason held the machine steady, ready to reduce the revs as soon as the load was removed.

In one neat movement David had the radio in his hands and was ducking out of the way of the whirling blades.

The manoeuvre completed, Jason brought the chopper down.

"Any problems?" he asked David.

"None my side. The radio slid off quite easily. How about you?"

"Everything went OK But I'd like to try it again just to make sure."

Jason took the Ranger up twice more and both times David was able to remove the radio without any problems.

That evening the boys met at Jason's. They were in his bedroom. David was sitting at the desk with a pad and pencil making careful notes, while Jason sat cross-legged on the floor. Mark sprawled on the bed, a stack of Jason's music tapes scattered about him.

"How much time d'you think you'll need to get the radio to Tessa?" David was working out a timetable.

Jason gnawed his lower lip. "Once the chopper's over the wall it shouldn't take longer than five minutes. But it'll take a few minutes to start the motor."

"You'll have to call us on the radio as soon as you're ready." Jason nodded his agreement.

David looked thoughtful. "But won't you need both hands on the chopper's transmitter? How can you talk on the radio at the same time?"

Jason had been concentrating on the chopper, he hadn't given much thought to using the radio. "You're right, Dave. I'm going to need one of you to help me communicate."

"I suppose that means I'm on my own distracting the crow and company," muttered Mark. "It'll probably take a bomb to get them out of the house."

Jason laughed. However, Mark had given him an idea. "Why don't we get hold of some fireworks. A few bangers should get them out. You know how sensitive these embassies are about being attacked. They'll think they're being fired at."

"I can do better than that," said Mark eagerly. "I'll make the bike backfire a few times as well. Then we can still go with the original plan and I'll make out that the bike went out of control and landed up under their gate. That should keep them out of your way for a while."

Jason was enthusiastic. But David asked, "What happens if they come out brandishing guns? Someone could get hurt."

"They wouldn't be able to see what was going on until they opened the gates. By that time I should be lying under the bike - harmless, no danger to anyone," said Mark.

"I hope you're right." David remembered previous wild schemes of Mark's which had not always worked out as planned.

"All the same, you'd better be careful," said Jason, feeling a certain responsibility for his friends' safety. They were only doing it for him.

David went through the plan step-by-step until they were all familiar with the procedure. They arranged to meet at Ocean Drive on Wednesday at 14h00.

Jason had to do some fast-talking to persuade Caitlin to drive him and the chopper down to Ocean Drive. However, a promise to spend the morning washing and cleaning her van finally won her over.

The boys were on time and by 14h30 the chopper and equipment were in place out of site behind the wall of 69.

Jason was tense with anxiety. A lot depended on his flying skills. He tried to relax; telling himself that everything was going to plan. The weather was good, with only a slight breeze blowing off the sea. There was no sign of the gardener, and there was no one on the balcony. "Have you got the fireworks?" he asked Mark.

"And matches?" added David.

"I managed to get half a dozen crackers. That should put the wind up them."

"Let's check the radios one more time," insisted David.

Mark rolled his eyes, he was impatient to get back to his bike and into position at the front of number 69.

They switched on the sets and scanned the visual displays to make sure all four radios were still tuned to the same frequency. "Do you copy?" Jason spoke into his radio. His voice echoed back from the other sets.

"They're OK I'm off. Over and out." Mark snapped off his radio.

"Good luck." Jason watched Mark jog back along the beach. "Be careful."

David moved into the shadow of the bushes and trained his binoculars on the balcony. "Coast's still clear."

A quarter of an hour later their radios came to life. "Mark to base. I'm in position. The road's clear. No one about."

Everything was ready. Now all they were waiting for was Tessa. Jason glanced at his watch. Five minutes to go. There was a flash of light from the balcony as the sun reflected off the glass of a French door as it opened.

"It's Tessa." David had been looking through his binoculars. Jason slipped out from behind the wall. He waited until she had seen him and then he signalled her to stay where she was. She gave him a thumbs-up. He and David got ready to start the chopper.

"Base to Mark. The show's on the road. Let the fireworks begin. Over and out," David spoke into the radio.

As soon as they heard the first bang, Jason fired the motor. He'd had to psyche himself up to stay calm. If they blew this, not only would it put Tessa in more danger, but it would also spoil their chances of any further attempts at communicating with her.

There were several more bangs as the chopper slowly rose into the air. Good, Mark was doing his stuff.

David kept the binoculars clamped to his eyes. "No sign of anyone else," he reported. "Although Tessa is looking a little confused."

But her face cleared when she saw the red and white chopper appear above the wall. As it rose over the electric fence and headed towards the house, she seemed to understand it was meant for her.

Keeping the machine a safe distance from the trees, Jason manoeuvred it towards the balcony. It was almost impossible to judge the clearance between the blades and the balcony railings, but he kept it as high as he dared without getting too close to the eaves. Tense with concentration, he told himself to relax, taking deep slow breaths.

Tessa had been watching the chopper's movements closely, waiting to see what he was up to.

There was a loud gunshot bang from the front of the house that signalled Mark's bike back-firing. It startled her, and for a moment drew her attention. But she quickly turned back. The chopper was now close enough for her to recognise the radio hanging beneath the skids.

But Mark's urgent voice came over the radio. "The front gate's opening. I think someone's coming out. What's happening your end?"

"Stall them," urged David. "We're about to deliver the goods. Over."

"Hurry it up."

Jason ran his tongue round his dry lips. He had the chopper hovering steadily above Tessa. She'd seen the radio. "Come on, Tessa, slide it off," he murmured. It was no use shouting instructions over the radio; she would not be able to hear above the noise of the motor. He needn't have worried. She seemed to know exactly what to do and reached up to take it.

But as her hand touched the wire loop, a sudden gust sent the chopper upward and off course. It was heading straight towards the overhanging eaves.

8

Jason's stomach did a flip. The chopper was heading for certain destruction. He had to act quickly to avert disaster. Instinctively he lowered the throttle speed. The chopper's lift was reduced and the pitch became less positive. He pulled back slightly on the cyclic control. The machine responded instantly, banking and heading away from the eaves. He let out a relieved breath.

"Break, break. They're going back towards the house." Mark sounded frantic.

"Try to stall them. Just a few more minutes," David urged.

Sweat trickled into Jason's eyes, but he dare not take his fingers off the controls. It was taking all his concentration to bring the machine round in a wide circle for a second approach at the balcony. Keep calm; don't try to hurry it, he told himself. Coolly he brought the chopper into position, adjusting the controls until it was hovering steadily.

Tessa was waiting. She wasted no time. Within seconds, the radio was in her hands. She waved and gave a thumbs-up before darting inside.

Jason wanted to give a whoop of delight, but he knew the danger wasn't over until the chopper was safely over the wall and out of sight. He could feel his T-shirt clinging damply to his back.

"Mission almost completed," David told Mark.

At first there was no response. Then David heard snatches of conversation. "It's OK. Don't worry. I'll get the bike going. Sorry to bother you." Mark had obviously pressed the transmit button to warn him that someone from the house was still there.

Then he heard a second voice. "Jason. Jason, are you there?" Tessa's voice was transmitting over both radios. Whoever was talking to Mark would also be able to hear her.

"Radio silence. Radio silence. Wait for instructions." David spoke quietly into the radio.

Jason heard the urgency in David's voice. Something was up. He had to get the chopper back quickly. Only a few more metres to go and it would be over the wall. But something was wrong. The chopper wasn't responding. It was starting to vibrate. A nut or bolt must have shaken loose. Oh no, not now. He fought to maintain height, praying that the vibrations wouldn't cause electrical interference. Then as the machine slowly responded he felt his taut muscles relax. He barely cleared the electrified fence on top of the wall before the chopper dropped onto the cushioned landing of dune vegetation.

Jason dropped down out of sight next to David. "What's happening? Let me speak to Tessa."

"Not yet. We have to wait to see if Mark's OK"

They could barely hear Mark's voice above the noise of his bike. "Heading back to Jason's. I think the neighbours have called the cops. I'll send Caitlin to fetch you. Over and out."

Jason didn't waste any time. He grabbed the radio. "Tessa, it's Jason. Can you talk?"

"Yes. Wait. I'll lock the bedroom door and switch on some music."

He felt his heart thud at the sound of her voice. Glancing at David, he let out a long breath. Maybe at last they were going to find out what was going on at 69 Ocean Drive.

"Jason, please. You've got to get in touch with my mother." She sounded desperate.

"I will. But what's going on, who's keeping you there?"

"My uncle."

"Your uncle! But why?"

"Look, I'd better tell you the whole story. My Uncle Carlos is head of the embassy."

"Must be the guy she was sitting with in the garden," whispered David.

"He's my father's younger brother. They are both Argentineans. But my mother's English. My parents met when my mother was piloting a small plane on my father's ranch in Argentina."

"Your mother's a pilot!" Jason and David exchanged looks.

"Small executive planes." Tessa was dismissive as she hurried to tell her story. "We lived on the ranch until my father was killed in a riding accident when I was eight. My mother and I went back to England. I didn't see my uncle again until last year when he suddenly turned up and invited me to the ranch for a holiday.

"Everything was great until about a month ago when he said he was taking me on a trip. He said he had okayed it with my mother. But when we got here he refused to let me speak to her."

Jason's mind whirled with questions. "But why is he keeping you here? Who are the others? Can't they do anything to help you?"

"Raul has worked for my uncle for years."

"And the woman?"

"She's my aunt. My father's sister. She was always jealous of my mother, and she hates me. She hardly lets me out of her sight." Jason could detect the bitterness in her voice.

"But why did your uncle kidnap you?" he persisted.

"I don't know. He won't tell me anything." She sounded frustrated. "But something weird is going on. There were a lot of Colombian visitors while we were in Argentina. I'm sure he's somehow involved with drugs."

Jason let out a low whistle. "But how would that involve you?"

"I don't know. I can't figure out what's going on. Jason, you've got to get in touch with my mother. She must be frantic wondering what's happened to me. She's the only one who can get me out of here."

"Give me her name and telephone number."

David wrote them down in the small notebook he kept for bird watching.

Jason wanted to go on talking to Tessa. There were still many unanswered questions. However, he realised Mark's appearance might have made the crow suspicious. They could be searching the grounds. It was best they got out. The most important thing now was to contact Tessa's mother.

"Tessa, I'll phone your mother as soon as I get home. I'll contact you on the radio again tonight."

"Make it at nine. My aunt will be watching the TV."

"Try to find out more about what your uncle is up to. But don't make them suspicious."

"Thanks, Jason. You seem to be my only hope." She sounded relieved that help might at last be on its way.

The boys headed back to where they'd arranged to meet Caitlin with the van. Mark was waiting with her. David climbed into the back with the chopper while Jason leapt into the front. He was expecting some awkward questions about what they had been up to. Instead, Caitlin was anxious to tell him her own news.

"Guess what?"

"What?" Jason tried to tear his thoughts away from Tessa.

"The college rang. That embassy you were talking about wants me to do the catering for their official reception."

"Are you sure? When is it? Did they ask you to supply waiters?" Jason had no trouble giving his sister his attention.

"Jason, slow down. What is it with you? Why is this reception so important?"

Jason fought with his conscience. Should he tell Caitlin the whole story? It would not only mean explanations about the chopper, but also the possibility of very real danger if, as Tessa suggested, drugs were involved. He doubted whether Caitlin would go along with their plans. She would probably insist on telling Mum and Dad. Besides, she'd have enough to worry about with the catering.

She kept glancing at him. "Why are you looking so worried? You haven't damaged the chopper, have you?"

"Not exactly," he hedged. "But it's playing up a bit. I might have to get the transmitter checked. You know how much that costs. I could do with some extra cash."

She smiled. "Well, you'll be glad to know I'll need three waiters. They want me to provide typical South African snacks. But they have their own catering staff for their traditional food."

"When is it?"

"Next week. Saturday. From four to seven."

Would Tessa's mother get here before Saturday? Surely she would fly straight out when she heard about her daughter. He wished Caitlin would put her foot down so he could get to the phone.

It seemed to take forever before the boys were piling out of the van. Mark was waiting for them. While Jason was putting the chopper away in the workshop he told them about the reception, and the chance it might give them to rescue Tessa.

"But surely she won't need rescuing if her mother gets here," said David.

"That's what I'm hoping," replied Jason.

Caitlin went straight to her room to plan the menu for the reception, so the boys had the phone to themselves.

Jason punched in the numbers in England that Tessa had given him. What was he going to say? How was he going to convince her mother he wasn't a raving nutter? "It's ringing."

It went on ringing.

"What's happening?" demanded Mark.

"There's no answer."

"Dial again. You might have dialled the wrong number," suggested David.

Jason tried again. "No one's picking up." This was something he hadn't counted on. He felt suddenly deflated.

"Try again in an hour."

Jason frowned. "I can't. I'm going to be late for my paper round." Not for the first time, he wished he didn't have to do it. "Dave, if you came with me I'd finish it quicker. And we could test the range of the radio, see if we can get Tessa from here. Mark, will you stay here and monitor it?"

"OK It'll give me a chance to go through your music tapes."

"We'll call you in about three-quarters of an hour. Don't forget to switch on."

Mark already had the tapes spread on Jason's bed.

When the boys reached Ocean Drive, Jason stopped the bike and killed the motor. "Let's hope Mark hasn't got too carried away with the music." Pulling off his helmet he pushed his hair out of his eyes and unclipped the radio from his waistband. "Jason to base. Come in Mark."

There was no answer.

"Maybe we're out of range," said David.

Jason glanced at his watch. "Let's give him a couple more minutes."

They were parked at the end of Ocean Drive, out of sight of number 69. "Come on, Mark," whispered Jason. If he could receive Tessa at home, maybe he could get her mother on the phone at the same time, and relay messages between them.

"Jason to base. Come in Mark."

"He's probably listening to the music through your headphones and can't hear." David always had a plausible explanation.

But this time he was wrong. In the next few seconds, Mark's voice came over clearly. "Base to Jason. D'you copy?"

Jason grinned and gave David a thumbs up. "Yeah, Mark. How well are you receiving me? Over."

"Well enough. The radio is registering four out of five. Over."

Jason checked his receiver. It was also registering four out of five, well within range. He was tempted to ask Mark to try the number in England again, but thought better of it. He wanted to be the one to speak to Tessa's mother. He couldn't afford for Mark to make a mess of things. "See you back at base in about half an hour. Over and out."

Back home, Jason tried the phone every half an hour until just before nine o'clock. It was clear that no one was at home. He felt as though he had let Tessa down.

At two minutes to nine, he switched on his radio.

"Jason are you there?" Tessa had been waiting. He felt his heart give a thump as he recognised that slight trace of an accent.

"Hi Tessa. I'm here."

"Did you get hold of her? Did you speak to my mother?"

"Tessa, I've tried all afternoon and evening. I'm sorry. There was no answer."

He could feel Tessa's disappointment as she asked, "Are you sure? Did you have the right number?"

He repeated it to her. He hadn't made a mistake.

"Where d'you think she could be? Is there anyone else we could try?"

"There're no other close relations in England except for my Gran, and she's in an old age home."

"What about in Argentina?"

"That's probably where my mother is now. She must have gone there looking for me."

"Is there no one there you trust?"

"Not now. They are all my uncle's relatives. I don't know what he's up to. He won't tell me anything. He won't tell me how long he's going to keep me here. I'm even doing a correspondence course under an assumed name so I won't miss any schooling. Jason, I've got to get out of here."

He could hear the desperation in her voice. "I'll keep trying to contact your mother. I'll get in touch with you again tomorrow at eleven. But if we can't contact her, there may be another way of getting you out."

"How? I've tried everything. My Aunt and Raul won't let me near the phone. And I have to stay in my room if we have visitors. There's a burglar alarm, and the fence is electrified."

"Think of Troy," said Jason mysteriously. "But we won't be coming in a wooden horse. We'll be in my sister's van."

"I don't understand. What do you mean?"

"My sister is doing the catering for your uncle's official reception next Saturday. My friends and I will be waiters."

"Jason, that could be dangerous. My uncle wouldn't let anything happen to me - but if Raul caught you or your friends... He's a dangerous man. I heard stories about him in Argentina."

Jason knew she was right. Guys like that didn't mess about. They'd already had a taste of what Raul could do that day on the beach. But he had to convince Tessa his plan would work. The trouble was - he didn't have an actual plan yet.

9

Jason had a sleepless night. The problems kept replaying in his mind. Would he be able to contact Tessa's mother? What was Tessa's uncle up to? How dangerous were the men who worked at the embassy? How would he get Tessa out of the house? He thrashed about in the sultry heat trying to fathom the answers. If Tessa's uncle wouldn't let her meet visitors, then she obviously wouldn't be at the reception. Would they be able to sneak her out over the balcony?

It was almost dawn when he finally slipped into an uneasy sleep.

When he woke it was with a dull feeling of depression. But he soon shook it off, and after showering and pulling on his favourite baggies and rhino T-shirt, went downstairs to the tempting smell of grilled bacon.

Mrs Hunter was dashing through the front door. It was her turn on the SPCA bookstand. "Your father phoned. He'll be home tomorrow," she said. She fled down the driveway to a waiting car, leaving the front door open for Striker, who was pondering indecisively on the doorstep.

Jason gathered up the cat and closed the door. He carried the purring bundle to the kitchen and opened a sachet of cat food into a dish before setting them both down on the floor. Caitlin glanced over her shoulder from the grilling bacon. "Dad'll be disappointed if he can't fly the helicopter. Will you be able to fix it?"

Jason had forgotten about the problem with the chopper. "I'll check it out after breakfast. But first, I have to make a phone call."

He closed the kitchen door, hoping the spitting eggs in the frying pan would muffle the sound of his conversation with Tessa's mother.

He knew the number almost by heart. England was an hour behind. If she were at home, surely she'd be in at seven in the morning.

As he heard the now familiar sound of the long distance call going through, he found his fist tightening round the receiver. There was a moment's silence before he heard the ringing tone. "C'mon. Be there," he murmured into the 'phone. But it simply went on ringing. Slowly he replaced the receiver. Damn, she must have gone to Argentina as Tessa suspected.

During breakfast, he quizzed Caitlin about the reception. "What are you giving them to eat? Have you decided?"

"It's a cocktail party so everything will be bite-size. I've thought about tiny biltong quiches, samoosas, chilli-bites, mini boerwors, melk tarts and koeksusters. I might even try something with crocodile meat. There'll also be dips and pates and things."

"How many people will you be catering for?" He sloshed a generous dollop of tomato sauce onto his eggs.

Caitlin frowned at the gooey mess on her brother's plate. "Would you like more eggs with your sauce?"

Jason grinned and spread some of the sauce onto his bacon. "Is it going to be a big reception?"

"About fifty guests."

"Local or foreign?"

"Both probably." She stopped buttering her toast. "Jason, I don't know what their guest list is. What difference does it make?"

"Sorry. Just showing an interest." He should have known better. She was always touchy when she was worried about a job.

They ate in silence for a few moments before she enquired in a kinder tone. "Have you asked Mark and David if they want to be waiters?"

"They never say no to some extra cash." He pushed back his chair and carried the dishes to the sink. When he had helped clear the table he told Caitlin he'd be in the workshop fixing the chopper.

He checked for loose parts, keeping his eye on his watch. He would try the phone a few more times before contacting Tessa at eleven.

It was some time before he found the problem with the chopper. A bolt had worked loose. Perhaps his Dad was right to go over them all and give them an extra turn. He took the machine into the garden and wiped it over with a soapy cloth. It had done its job. Now it was ready again for his Dad to fly.

Caitlin gave him a cheery wave as she went down the drive. Now would be a good time to try the phone again.

There was still no reply. It looks increasingly like a lost cause, thought Jason resignedly. It looked as though the reception would be their only hope of rescuing Tessa.

At two minutes to eleven, Jason switched on his radio. "Tessa, are you there?"

She was waiting. "Hi Jason. Have you heard anything from my mother?"

He could hear the faint hope in her voice. He felt awful having to let her down. "I'm sorry. It looks as though you were right. She must be in Argentina."

"Well, thanks for trying," she sighed.

"I'll keep phoning, just in case. Did you find out anything about what your uncle is up to?"

"Not much. I overheard Raul on the phone. But he was talking in Spanish and too fast for me to understand everything."

"What did you hear?"

"It sounded like a consignment being due on the seventeenth."

"The seventeenth. That's the day of the reception."

"I know. I wondered if he was talking about wine."

"I doubt it. Keep listening, you may hear more. But Tessa - watch out. I'll contact you again tonight at nine."

"Thanks, Jason. I really appreciate what you're doing. I think I'll go mad if I don't get out of here."

Her voice made his heart thud. "Don't thank me until we have got you out. I'll speak to you again at nine."

He needed a plan to get Tessa out. Maybe Mark and David would have some ideas.

The beach was crowded. As he was weaving his way through the lines of sizzling bodies, Jason tried hard not to resent the invasion of the holidaymakers.

He could see Mark talking to one of the lifeguards. But who was the girl with him? He couldn't see her face, but the colour and style of her hair was enough to make his heart gallop - but there was no way it could be Tessa!

The girl threw back her head and laughed, punching Mark playfully on the shoulder. When she turned, Jason saw at once that it was Nicole. He let out a breath that was at once relief and disappointment. Why hadn't he noticed before that the resemblance went further than similar hair colouring?

He sprinted the last few metres. A plan was beginning to take shape in his mind.

"Hey, Jason. Just in time for Cokes." Mark pulled another can out of the cooler bag.

"Thanks. Where's David?"

"He's borrowed my board. Why?"

"I need to talk to you both."

"Why? Has something happened about Tessa?"

"Who's Tessa?" broke in Nicole.

"Nothing to do with nosy kids like you." Mark pressed the cold Coke can on her bare back.

She squealed and threw a punch at him. But he was too quick and ducked out of her way. "You'll be sorry, brush head," she threatened.

"C'mon you two, this is serious." Jason drew Mark away from the crowd. They found a shady spot on the grassed bank and sat down while Jason put his idea to Mark, who was all for it. But when a dripping David joined them he carefully thought it through while he towelled himself. "It's feasible - but it's also dangerous. And there is a lot that depends on Nicole. D'you think she'd even want to help?"

Mark finger-combed his hair. "Nicole is game for most things. But when it comes to helping someone - it depends who's doing the asking." He grinned slyly at Jason.

Jason felt the blood creeping up his face. There had been a time when Nicole's crush had been very obvious. "I'll ask her. But we'll have to make it clear she's not to tell anyone else."

Half an hour later an initially dubious Nicole had agreed to take part in their plan.

"Caitlin got the embassy job," Mrs Hunter, gently lifting the cat off her lap, told her husband at breakfast the following morning,

Mr Hunter glanced at his daughter as he poured cornflakes into his bowl. "Is that the job that Jason was so keen on?"

"Yes. There will probably be some important people there. Jason is going to be on his best behaviour - aren't you, Jason?"

"What?" Jason had been going over the plan in his mind and the conversation had drifted over his head.

"Next Saturday. The reception. Best behaviour!"

"Sure," agreed Jason guiltily, knowing that what he had in mind was far from what Caitlin would see as `best behaviour'.

"But next Saturday is the seventeenth," said Mr Hunter. "What time does this reception begin?"

"It's from four till seven. Why?" asked Caitlin.

He turned to Jason. "It's the finish of the cross-Africa air race. I thought we were going to watch it. Had you forgotten?"

Jason's stomach felt as though it had suddenly dropped through a pocket of turbulence. Since he'd met Tessa everything else seemed to have been swept from his mind. "Is the race really next Saturday?"

"It's on all the posters. You've known about it for weeks. They're expecting the first plane home at about three-thirty."

"Sorry, Dad. I guess I'll have to miss it."

Jason saw the disappointment in his Dad's face, and so, apparently, had his mother. "Perhaps Caitlin could find someone else to be a waiter," she suggested.

The panic in Jason's face mirrored his sister's. "Jason knows how I work. I don't like the idea of training anyone new for such an important function." But when she saw her father's face, she added, "I suppose I could get one of the college students to help."

Jason's grip tightened round his spoon. He had to be at that reception. "Dad, I can't let Caitlin down. Not for such an important job."

"But you were so keen to see the air race."

"I was... I am... But I know how much this job means to Cait."

Caitlin gave her brother a puzzled frown. Even Mrs Hunter looked confused.

Mr Hunter shrugged. "It's your decision. But it'll probably be another five years before the race finishes here again."

Jason felt his grip relax. "I know. And I'll be sorry to miss it. But I have promised Caitlin."

Mr Hunter reached for the toast rack and took out a slice of toast. "How's the chopper? I believe you've had it out. Why don't we take it down to the field later."

Jason hesitated. He and Tessa had got into the habit of contacting each other at 11 am and 9 p.m. every day. "Can we be back by eleven? I have to make a phone call."

Mr Hunter spread a neat layer of butter over his toast. "If you like."

Caitlin chuckled. "It must be his mystery girlfriend."

Mrs Hunter's eyebrows disappeared under her perm. "We haven't heard about..." she began, but hesitated when she caught Jason's pleading eyes."I'm sure we'll meet Jason's new friend when he sees fit," she said, pouring the milk into the teacups.

Jason shot his mother a grateful glance. Now was not the time to be answering awkward questions.

Straight after breakfast, Jason and his father set off for the flying club. The chopper performed beautifully, and much to Jason's relief, at twenty minutes to eleven they were pulling up in the driveway.

He phoned Mark briefly to see how the arrangements for the rescue plan were progressing. Then he dialled Tessa's mother; in what he was beginning to realise was a futile effort. He put down the phone and slipped into his room to contact Tessa.

This time she didn't ask whether he'd got through to England. She told him eagerly, "My aunt let something slip. She said `when your mother gets here'. I tried to pump her for more information, but she realised she'd said too much and clammed up. Jason, I don't know what's going on, but maybe when my mother gets here the whole thing will be cleared up."

"Let's hope so," said Jason. But he had his doubts. Once Tessa's mother was inside the embassy she could also become a prisoner. And there would be nothing anyone could do about it.

10

The boys spent the following week working on the details of their plan. From the information Tessa gave them they were able to draw a fairly detailed map of the house. There were four bedrooms upstairs, two with en-suite bathrooms, two sharing a guest bathroom. There was also a TV lounge, which with two of the bedrooms, including Tessa's, led off the balcony. Downstairs was the master bedroom with an adjoining office used by Tessa's uncle. There was also the formal lounge, dining room, kitchen, and a guest cloakroom close to the front entrance.

They felt certain that Tessa would be kept in her room, possibly locked in, during the reception.

"What about the door to the balcony? Could we get her out that way?" Mark pointed out the possibility as they pored over the plan that was spread on Jason's desk.

"Even if the door weren't locked, we'd still have to sneak her off the balcony," replied Jason.

"Knotted sheets?"

"Too risky," said David. There's bound to be people wandering about the garden."

"Then we'll have to find some way of unlocking the door. Perhaps Tessa will know where the keys are kept." Jason chewed his lower lip thoughtfully.

"I've got a better idea," said Mark. "My Dad knows a lot of people in the security business. There're gadgets for opening locks."

Jason looked at him eagerly. "Can you get hold of one?"

"Shouldn't be a problem," shrugged Mark.

David ticked his list. "Has Nicole got the clothes?"

"I sneaked them out of Caitlin's room. I doubt if she'll miss them." Jason glanced at the list. "Looks like we've done all we can. I'll explain everything to Tessa tonight."

"You'll all be taking a big risk," warned Tessa.

"We don't have a choice," said Jason.

Tessa was silent for a few moments. He knew she was desperate to get out. She would have to agree. "Watch out for Raul. His job is security. He might recognise you."

"I'll keep my head down."

During the rest of the week Tessa continued to feed them information gleaned from overheard conversations. But none of it made the puzzle any clearer.

"They're definitely expecting something on the seventeenth. And Raul is going to pick it up," said Tessa. "That means it will probably be coming by sea or air. He said it was due around five this evening, so it seems more likely that he'll be meeting an international flight."

"That sounds feasible." Jason had the radio hunched between ear and shoulder as he lay on his bed, his voice low in case Caitlin or his mother walked past his door. "Perhaps they're smuggling something in the diplomatic bag."

"Then what do they need me for?"

"That's the part I can't figure. Look, I'll check on the international flights expected at five. It might give us a clue if we know which country the flight is coming from."

However, Jason didn't have much luck. There were no international flights expected at that time.

On the morning of the seventeenth Jason woke early with a feeling of nervous anticipation. Through the wall he could hear the shower running in the bathroom he shared with Caitlin. She was also anxious about the outcome of this afternoon's reception - but for very different reasons.

While he was dressing he wondered when would be the best time to speak to Caitlin about Nicole. He would have to make sure his sister was in a receptive mood.

He watched her during breakfast, frowning as she sprinkled sugar on her muesli. She looked jumpy and unapproachable. She'd need softening up.

"D'you want any help with the preparations? Any last minute things from the market?" he asked, buttering his toast.

Three pairs of questioning eyes swivelled in his direction.

"What's wrong? I'm just trying to help."

"Nothing's wrong," said Mrs Hunter.

Jason saw his parents exchange glances.

"You can help me load the van later on," suggested Caitlin, scraping her chair as she got up to fetch the teapot.

"Oh, by the way," said Jason, "David might not be able to make it this afternoon. Is it all right if Nicole takes his place?"

Jason heard the sharp intake of breath as his sister swung round. "Nicole!"

"Yes, Nicole. She'll make a good waitress. She's got a nice smile, and she's polite." Jason found himself groping for excuses. Nicole was vital to their plan. Caitlin had to agree. "And she's had experience."

"What sort of experience?" Caitlin looked dubious.

"She's helped out a couple of afternoons serving tea and scones at the charity kiosk."

"Not quite the same thing," said Caitlin. But she hadn't said no, and she seemed to be considering the idea as she poured the tea into the cups.

Jason took advantage of her silence to press his point. "She can borrow your waitress's apron and cap. She'll be OK It's not as though it's a sit-down meal."

"You've left it very late. Why didn't you tell me earlier? I might have been able to get an experienced waiter."

"David only told me last night," lied Jason.

"I suppose it'll be all right." Caitlin handed out the tea, her face already creasing with worry.

Jason tried not to let his relief show. Another part of the plan was in place.

After breakfast he rode over to pick up David and they both went on to Mark's. Caitlin's black skirt, white blouse, apron and cap were in his backpack.

"Where's the clothes I gave you earlier?" he asked Nicole, dropping the bag on the kitchen table.

"Don't worry. They're all packed and ready." She flashed him a cheeky smile.

"This isn't a game, Nicole," he said sternly, concerned about her casual attitude.

Mark was making cheese and chutney sandwiches. "Want some?" He offered the plate to the boys. They both declined. He folded one in half and stuffed it into his mouth, extending the buttery knife to Fluffy, one of Nicole's cats, which had taken up an anticipatory stance on the counter.

"Isn't that unhygienic?" David frowned as the pink tongue hungrily licked the traces of butter.

"Dishwasher sterilises it." Mark flung the licked knife into the sink, which would mean someone else having to retrieve it and put it into the dishwasher.

"You didn't ask me if I wanted any," said Nicole petulantly.

"Make your own."

Jason saw Nicole's eyes flash. Now was not the time to get on the wrong side of her. Fluffy was delicately washing her whiskers. He scooped up the purring bundle of fur and stroked her gently under the chin. "Hey, Nicole, she's putting on weight."

"No she's not." Nicole was instantly distracted. Her face softened. "She's just right." Lifting the cat out of Jason's arms, she snuggled it into her neck.

"Let's sit down and run through the arrangements." Jason pulled out a kitchen chair and they settled down at the scrubbed wooden table.

They recited their parts in turn. Each knew what they had to do. There was a feeling of excitement, as if they were setting out on a risky adventure holiday, like white-water rafting, or mountaineering. An excitement tinged with fear. But they realised this could be Tessa's only chance. They couldn't afford to mess it up. At least Nicole now seemed to be taking the whole thing seriously.

"And David will be waiting at the end of Ocean Drive with my scrambler," concluded Jason. "I don't want to get caught driving the van without a licence. It might take too much explaining."

"If David drives it back to 69, won't it look suspicious? A white guy drives it out, and then a black guy drives in?" said Mark.

"It's a risk we'll have to take. But Tessa should be safely out by then," replied Jason.

They arranged for Mark and Nicole to be at Jason's at two-thirty that afternoon.

At two-fifteen, Jason was still fumbling with his bow tie. Last minute disasters were flashing through his mind. Petrol. Had he remembered to fill the scrambler's tank? Spare helmet for Tessa? Would David remember it? Tessa's door. What if they couldn't unlock it? He tried to dismiss these fears and think positively.

The van was loaded, but he could hear Caitlin in the kitchen opening and closing cupboard doors as she re-checked her list.

Then Mark's bike was roaring up the drive. One final glance in the mirror to make sure the bow tie was straight, and he was bounding down the stairs.

Nicole was wearing the black skirt and crisp white blouse of the waitress's uniform. The apron and cap were in her bag, together with the clothes for Tessa.

"Everything ready?"

Mark gave him a thumbs up.

Jason and Nicole sat in the front of the van with Caitlin, while Mark found a space between the boxes and trays of food at the back.

Fifteen minutes later the van was drawing up at the gates of 69. Jason rang the bell. "Catering." He spoke sharply in case anyone recognised his voice.

The gates swung open. It was the first time he'd had a good look at the front of the house. On the left, he recognised the windows that would be Tessa's uncle's office and master bedroom. On the right was the dining room. The drive swept up to the front door between neatly clipped hibiscus bushes, and round to the side. As they approached the front door it swung open and a figure appeared in the doorway. Jason kept his head down in case it was Raul or the crow. But it was one of the lackeys come to tell them to drive round to the back.

Caitlin pulled on the creaking handbrake. "Jason, you and Mark unload the van." Nerves were making her sharp. She disappeared into the kitchen to inspect the facilities. It was spacious and had been recently modernised with country-style oak cupboards. There were two ovens and a microwave. Beneath the window, which overlooked a walled courtyard, an elderly woman was clattering dishes in a foaming sink. She glanced up at the newcomers through narrowed eyes, put out at the invasion of her domain.

Jason carried in a tray of snacks. "Keep that bag close to you," he whispered to Nicole. "We've got to get the clothes upstairs later."

She nodded, and after taking out her apron and cap, placed the bag on a shelf under the large rectangular worktable which dominated the centre of the kitchen.

Jason was desperate to get a look at the rest of the house, and mostly to let Tessa know he was there. But he couldn't afford to bump into the crow, Raul, or Tessa's uncle. He'd have to wait until he could mingle with the guests.

The elderly woman finished at the sink and turned her attention to an olive-skinned young man who was pulling a tray out of the oven. Hot, spicy smells filled the room.

Caitlin introduced herself, and the woman reluctantly cleared several platters of food to make a working space on a counter next to the huge fridge. Caitlin showed Nicole how she wanted the *koeksusters* and *melk tarts* arranged on platters, and then turned to supervise Jason and Mark who were stacking trays on the counter. As they loaded the final tray the kitchen door swung open. To Jason's horror, the crow swept in. Mark had also seen her. He turned his back and bent over a tray of mini quiches. Jason ducked and peered intently through the glass door of the oven.

However, Nicole had no qualms. "Good afternoon." She offered the woman a *koeksuster.*

Jason and Mark exchanged alarmed glances. But the crow shook her head, declining the syrupy confection. She spoke sharply in Spanish to the elderly woman, and then turned on her heel and marched out. The elderly woman muttered a few words over her shoulder as the door closed. They obviously aren't the best of friends, thought Jason letting out a deep breath of relief.

The young man began taking the wine and the glasses through to the dining room where the bar had been set up. Jason offered to help. He followed along a small passage that led into the tiled main entrance. A stone pedestal stood by the door. On it was a porcelain vase with red and yellow chrysanthemums. A wide sweeping staircase with polished wooden banisters led to the upstairs rooms. On the left, the dining room door stood open. Opposite was the guest cloakroom. Next to it, with the door slightly ajar, was the office. Tessa's uncle was seated behind the desk. An ornate ceiling fan whirred above his head. If he glanced up he would see anyone going up the stairs. Jason decided it would be too risky to try the stairs for the moment.

At 4 o'clock, the guests began arriving. Jason recognised the Mayor, looking flushed in a suit, and several local businessmen. The crow was acting as hostess. Jason kept out of her way as she ushered the ladies into the formal lounge.

He noticed that the driveway gates had been left open, and when he glanced out of the window he saw Raul checking the cars as they arrived. They weren't taking any chances on gatecrashers.

By 4.15 p.m. the lounge was beginning to fill and people were spilling into the garden.

"We've got to get some of them upstairs," muttered Jason, as he and Mark politely offered the trays of cocktails to the mingling guests. "I think it's time I put the sign up."

He went to the kitchen and nodded a signal to Nicole. She was arranging hot *boerwors* between tiny *biltong* pizzas, her face flushed with the heat. She glanced round to make sure no one was watching before ducking beneath the table and bringing out a small cardboard sign from her bag. Jason slipped it under his tray and made his way to the guest cloakroom. Making sure there was no one about, he slipped inside. He quickly propped the sign on the toilet seat. OUT OF ORDER. PLEASE USE UPSTAIRS CLOAKROOM. Opening the door again he glanced out. The crow was greeting two elegantly dressed ladies at the entrance. He ducked back inside and waited a few moments before trying again. The women were disappearing into the lounge with a waft of expensive perfume.

"Ply them all with drinks." Jason grinned as he passed Mark in the kitchen.

It was not long before some of the guests began trekking up the stairs.

"It's time," Jason whispered to Nicole, who was wiping crumbs from the counter. They glanced at Caitlin. She was putting quiches in the oven, brushing stray wisps of hair from her eyes with the back of her hand in a harassed manner.

Nicole pulled out the package of clothes. She folded them as flat as possible so that Jason could slip them under the tray of hot cocktails. He slid a second tray under the first.

Caitlin suddenly swung round. "Serve these while they're still hot." She turned back to lift the quiches out of the oven, tendrils of hair damp over her forehead.

Jason dutifully transferred several of the quiches to his tray. Nicole gave him a discreet wink as he left.

He checked on the crow and Tessa's uncle. They were safely mingling with the guests in the lounge. He could hear snatches of Spanish followed by the crow's shallow laughter.

He made for the stairs. A few people had discovered the upstairs balcony and were admiring the sea view. He offered them snacks in case anyone asked what he was doing up there.

Soon he was heading down the passage towards Tessa's door. As his feet sank into the thick-piled carpet, he could feel his heart pumping. He tapped on her door and waited, his head thudding.

11

"Tessa. It's me, Jason."

"Jason. Thank goodness. The door. It's locked."

Jason had already taken the lock-picking gadget out of his pocket and was fitting it into the keyhole. "I think I can get it open," he whispered through the door, listening as the tumblers vibrated. He kept checking the passage in case anyone going into the lounge glanced his way.

His hands were sweaty with anxiety. It seemed an age before he heard the lock click. Swiftly he opened the door and ducked inside.

Tessa was suddenly before him. His breath caught in his throat as her anxious hazel eyes stared into his own. He wanted more than anything to take her in his arms. But now wasn't the time.

She took his hand. "Jason, I've found out what's going on. They're blackmailing my mother."

"Blackmailing... how?"

"There's a cross-Africa air race. It ends here this afternoon."

"I know," broke in Jason. "It finishes at the small airfield used by private planes. But how is your mother involved?"

"She's taking part in the race. They've packed her plane with cocaine. They've threatened that if she doesn't bring it through she will never see me again. We've got to get to the airfield."

"Wow. So that's what they're up to." Jason thought quickly. He glanced at his watch. "Some of the planes will already have landed. There's no time to try to convince the police. Come on, we've got to get you out, and then get to that cocaine before Raul. Once it's in his car, technically it will be on foreign soil and the police won't be able to touch him. Here are the clothes," he said, handing her the package. "Quick, put them on. We haven't much time."

Tessa raced into the bathroom and scrambled into them.

"Brush your hair a little more forward over your face," he said as she put on the cap.

They each picked up a tray. Jason carefully opened the door.

"I'll go first. When you see my signal - follow."

There were a few people chattering in the TV lounge, but no sign of the crow, Raul, or Tessa's uncle. Tessa was behind him when he reached the stairs.

"I'll check the entrance. If it's clear, make for the cloakroom and lock the door while I see if the kitchen's safe."

There was no one near the entrance. He could see Tessa's uncle and the crow talking animatedly to guests in the lounge. He signalled to Tessa. She hurried down the stairs and towards the cloakroom. However, before she could open the door, Raul appeared from the office. "Where's she going?"

Keeping her back to him, Tessa swiftly pushed open the door and darted inside.

"There're staff quarters at the back. You should have been told to use those."

"Sorry," muttered Jason. Raul gave him a quizzical look, as if he remembered him from somewhere. Jason kept his head down, his eyes fixed on the tray. His heart felt as though it were jumping out of his chest as he walked swiftly to the kitchen.

Nicole was on her own. She looked up enquiringly. "What's happening?"

"Tessa's in the cloakroom. We've got to get to the airfield." He gave her a quick outline of the story. "Where's Caitlin?"

"Putting some boxes in the van to clear more space."

"We'll have to get her out of the way while we sneak Tessa out."

Mark breezed in with an empty tray. "What a lot of gannets. There's going to be no food left for us."

"Mark," said Jason urgently. "Tessa's in the downstairs cloakroom. We've got to get her through the kitchen to the van. But Caitlin's out there. Tell her the crow wants to see her about something."

Caitlin wore a worried look as she hurried through the kitchen wiping her hands on her apron. There wouldn't be much time before she realised there'd been a mistake. Jason went quickly to the cloakroom and tapped on the door. "Tessa, hurry."

The door swung open and they darted down the passage and into the kitchen.

Nicole was waiting outside by the van. "Good luck," she whispered as Jason bundled Tessa into the back.

"Thanks." She squeezed Nicole's hand as Jason was closing the door.

He jumped into the driver's seat and slammed the door. They had to get away before Caitlin came back. But when he went to turn on the ignition the keys were missing. Damn, what had she done with them? He could feel his heart knocking in his chest as he raced back to the kitchen. "Nicole - the keys," he hissed. "Where are they?"

Nicole looked up in alarm. "I don't know."

Don't panic, Jason told himself. Try her bag, that's the most obvious place. It was on the shelf under the table next to Nicole's. "Watch the door," he called to Nicole. He fumbled through the bag until with relief his hand touched the cold metal of the keys.

"Hurry," yelled Nicole. "Caitlin's coming back."

Jason sprinted out of the door and was back in the driver's seat as an angry Caitlin strode into the kitchen arguing volubly with Mark.

Through the window in the back of the cab Jason signalled to Tessa to keep her head down. He started the motor, threw the van into gear, and headed for the gates.

There were several cars parked on the driveway and between the bushes on the lawns. Jason had only driven the van a few times, and never on public roads. His hands were damp on the steering wheel as he guided it between the parked cars.

Raul had left one of his lackeys to guard the gate. Fortunately, it was open. Jason gave the man a curt wave as the van sped through.

As he headed down Ocean Drive he allowed his grip to relax on the wheel. Tessa was free. But he couldn't afford to become complacent. They still had to get to the airfield before Raul.

David was waiting with the bike. Jason pulled up and opened the van doors. Tessa scrambled out. She took off the apron and cap, tossing her hair free.

"You must be David." She extended a slender hand. "Thanks for all your help."

David gave her a warm smile and handed her the helmet. "That's OK."

"Dave, we've got to get to the airfield." Jason yanked off his bow tie as he explained.

David let out a low whistle, "So that's what there're up to."

"No one must know Tessa is missing. With a bit of luck, you'll get the van back before Caitlin realises it's gone." He donned the helmet and swung his leg over the saddle.

Tessa hitched up her skirt and climbed on behind him.

"Hold tight," said Jason, gunning the engine. He felt her arms snaking round his waist. His breath caught in his throat as he felt her body pressed snugly against him.

He yelled to David, "Tell Caitlin I'll explain everything later. See you back at my place." He slipped the bike into gear and roared off towards the airfield.

The noise of the bike made it impossible to talk, and Jason needed all his concentration to get to the airfield as quickly as possible without being caught for speeding.

The air race had attracted a large crowd. There was no parking left for cars. Even the verges outside the perimeter fence were stacked with vehicles. But he was able to get to the main gate on the bike.

There was an entrance fee. Would he have enough for the two of them? He rifled through his pockets. With his loose change, he just made it.

He headed for the area where the planes were landing, but a parking attendant waved him to the other end of the car park.

He slewed the bike to a stop. They pulled off their helmets. "Come on, let's go." He took Tessa's hand and they ran towards the planes. He knew his father must be somewhere in the crowd. But there would be no time to explain.

They made for the main building where he expected the pilots would be taken for customs clearance and passport checks. A camera crew in a roped off area was interviewing the pilots for a local TV station.

"It doesn't look as though your mother is in yet. Do you know what sort of plane she'll be flying?"

"I know what she uses for stunt flying, and commercial flying. But I'm not sure what she'll use for a race."

The P.A. system was relaying information from air traffic control. From what they could make out there were two planes approaching the airfield, ten minutes apart.

They elbowed their way through the crowd until they found a space against the barrier rail erected to keep the spectators off the runway. "The programme should have a list of the planes and their pilots," said Jason. He turned to an elderly man standing next to him. "Excuse me, sir. Do you mind if I have a look at your programme?"

The man smiled and handed the programme to Jason. He and Tessa eagerly scanned the list of pilots. "That's her." Tessa's finger rested on the name. "Samantha Barrea. She's flying a Beechcraft. Like the one over there." She pointed to the low-wing plane parked beside the hangar.

Jason was impressed. "Do you know much about these planes?"

"A fair amount. My mother often takes me up with her." She glanced at her watch. "Raul said he had an appointment at 5.15 p.m. It's nearly that now. They must have planned what time she would get in. Let's see if we can get some information from the control tower."

But the tower was off-limits. They would have to rely on the announcements.

"Let's get as close as we can to the hangar," said Jason. "That's where they'll be unloading luggage." There was a fenced viewing area close by, with thatched umbrellas, table, and chairs. Waiters were serving drinks. It had obviously been reserved for the dignitaries.

"We'll never get in there," muttered Jason.

"Yes we will," said Tessa determinedly. She strode over to the man guarding the entrance. "Excuse me. I'm Tessa Barrea. My mother is a pilot in the race. Will it be all right if we watch from here until she comes in?"

The man looked doubtful at first. But Tessa's smile eventually won him over. "OK, but don't tell anyone I let you in."

"Come on." She grinned at Jason. They stood leaning over the fence, earnestly listening to the announcements. The Beechcraft piloted by Samantha Barrea was one of the two planes expected within the next fifteen minutes.

"We'd better keep a lookout for Raul." Jason looked over the crowd towards the car park entrance. The embassy probably had reserved parking. However, as he finished speaking, Tessa gave a gasp of dismay. He swung round. Standing in the doorway was Raul - and he had seen Tessa.

12

By the time Jason turned back, Tessa had vaulted the fence.

"Tessa," he called out, but she was already racing towards the hangar. He bounded the fence and sprinted after her. He saw her climb onto the Beechcraft's wing and pull open the door.

He was close behind and when he reached the plane he glanced over his shoulder. Raul's tall figure was forcing its way through the crowd.

"Tessa, what are you doing?" he shouted as he leapt onto the wing. She was in the pilot's seat, already freeing the control lock.

"Jason, get in and close the door."

"But Tessa," he spluttered, clambering in beside her, "you're not going to try to fly this thing?"

"It's our only chance." She flicked the battery switch.

He glanced out of the window. Raul was racing towards them. "Are you sure you know what you're doing? Have you flown in one of these before?"

"Not this model, but my mother had a Cessna. She used to let me take over the controls," she replied, priming the engine.

She turned the key and the motor fired. The prop started spinning. "You'd better hurry," he shouted. Raul was closing in on them.

She checked the windsock and headed for the runway. As they began taxiing out, she flicked the radio switch.

The control tower crackled over the radio. "Mike, Juliet, Romeo. What are your intentions?"

"Don't answer them yet," said Tessa.

They were picking up speed. Jason turned to see where Raul was. He'd given up the chase. When Jason turned back, he saw that Tessa was gripping the controls in fierce concentration.

The radio crackled again. This time the voice was more urgent. "Mike, Juliet, Romeo. What are your intentions? Mike, Juliet, Romeo, come in. You are not cleared for take off."

But the plane was speeding down the runway. He watched Tessa going through the take-off procedure. He knew the routine from his model flying. She seemed to know what she was doing.

The ground was flashing past. As they picked up more speed it seemed they were aimed straight for the bush at the edge of the airfield. He felt his jaw tightening and he braced himself for the sickening crash. He wanted to close his eyes, but he felt like a rabbit caught in headlights. Then there was a slight jar as they lifted into the air. "Phew!" he said, with a sigh of relief.

Soon they were banking and heading out over the sea. Over the radio he could hear the control tower warning the other pilots to keep away from the airfield.

They completed the ascent and Tessa reduced the power, mixture, and pitch controls to cruise settings. "How many times have you flown solo?" Jason steeled himself for the reply.

"This is the first time."

He gave a sharp intake of breath. "I hope you can get us down as easily as you got us up."

She scanned the controls, and noticing the green lights telling them that the undercarriage was still down, flipped the switch. Soon the red light indicated that the wheels had safely retracted.

"I'll circle over the sea."

The control tower was still trying to make contact. Jason picked up the microphone that was clipped to the armrest. "This is Mike, Juliet, Romeo. I'm Jason Hunter. The pilot is Tessa Barrea. Her mother is taking part in the air race. We have reason to believe her plane is packed with cocaine."

There was a brief silence before the control tower replied. "Mike, Juliet, Romeo. Return to the airfield. You are endangering other aircraft. You are clear to land on runway zero five."

"They're not listening," said Jason furiously.

"We'll stay up here until they do listen."

Jason pressed the mike button. "We're staying up until we can talk to the customs, and someone from the police narcotics division."

Tessa had turned the plane and they were heading back along the coast parallel with the airfield.

The control tower was silent.

"They must be discussing what they are going to do about us," said Jason.

Then the tower replied. "The customs men are in the building. But it may take some time to get through to the narcotics people."

"We just want to make sure you take us seriously."

They could hear the control tower instructing the other pilots to keep circling the airfield.

"Jason, you have to make them believe you. We don't have much time," urged Tessa.

Jason looked at her sharply. "Why not?"

"Fuel. We are very low. That's probably why the plane was parked outside the hangar. It was waiting to be re-fuelled."

"How much time do we have?"

Her face was grim. "Minutes."

Then the customs officer came on. "Mike Juliet Romeo. This is First Customs Officer Reynolds. Repeat your message concerning the cocaine."

Jason briefly relayed the story, describing Raul and emphasising the urgency of keeping him away from the plane. "If he gets the cocaine into the car you won't be able to touch him."

There was radio silence while the customs officer digested this information.

Jason could see the needles fluttering on the fuel gauges. The man had to believe him.

Finally, the customs officer replied. "When the plane lands we'll keep everyone away until we've inspected it."

Jason let out a relieved breath. He turned to Tessa. "You can take us down."

Her face was set in concentration. She banked and they began the descent towards the airfield.

"Mike, Juliet, Romeo. You are clear to land on runway zero five," instructed the control tower. "Wind one zero degrees. One to two knots."

Jason watched Tessa setting the approach flaps and re-setting the power, pitch and mixture controls, recognising some of the procedure from his model flying. They began their descent. She throttled back until the rev counter entered the green arc area. They were down to 500 feet. The fuel needles were now steady on empty. He tried not to think about what would happen if the engine cut. They were almost there. The fence at the edge of the airfield flashed into view. Tessa selected full flap for the landing. They passed over the fence at 100 feet. She cut the throttle. Suddenly a warning horn screamed.

"The undercarriage," cried Tessa.

Jason saw the red light directly in front of him. He snapped the switch. Nothing happened. The horn continued to scream. "It's stuck." He could see the faces of the crowd. "Pull up. Do another circuit," he yelled.

"No time. No fuel. Try it again," shouted Tessa.

They were over the runway. If she didn't pull up they would overshoot. He tried the switch again. Nothing. He tried again. This time, to his relief, the three green lights appeared telling him that the wheels had dropped.

Almost immediately he felt the slight bump as they touched the tarmac. But they were going too fast, heading off the tarred runway onto the grassed area. The grass seemed to slow them and the plane came to a stop a few metres before the bush, the engine still running.

Neither of them spoke. Then Jason said quietly, "We made it." The sense of relief was enormous. He turned to Tessa. She was grinning. On impulse he leaned towards her and briefly their lips met.

In a short time they were taxiing back to the hangar.

A cluster of officials was waiting for them, and an irate-looking man who was obviously the plane's owner. Tessa flicked the rudder and the plane headed for the parking area. However, ten metres short, the engine gave a final splutter and died. The fuel tanks had finally dried up. It was only then that they realised how close it had been. For a few moments they stared at each other, numb with relief.

Then a uniformed figure was standing on the wing opening the door. "You kids have a lot of explaining to do."

Tessa switched everything off and they scrambled out and watched the plane being pushed to safety.

"Come on," said the uniformed man, ushering them towards the main building. "We want to interview you in the manager's office."

"But we've got to be here when Tessa's mother lands," protested Jason. "She has to see that Tessa is safe."

"We'll take you out to meet the plane when it lands," the man assured them.

Then a figure extracted itself from the crowd. "What the heck is going on?"

"Dad!" Jason didn't know whether to be relieved or alarmed. His father might be more difficult to convince than the police and customs.

In the manager's office Jason let Tessa do most of the talking. At least everyone now seemed to be taking them seriously.

"If we do find cocaine we'll call in the police," said the custom's officer.

The phone shrilled. "Your mother's plane is approaching the airfield."

Jason took Tessa's hand and they raced out of the building towards the approach strip. The plane was circling overhead. He could feel the tension in Tessa and gave her hand a reassuring squeeze. There was no sign of Raul.

The plane headed downwind and began its descent.

"I hope you're right about all this," said Mr Hunter, coming up behind them. "Theft of an aeroplane is a serious business."

But Jason had no time to reply. The plane had touched down. When it had almost reached the end of the runway it turned and headed towards them. Suddenly Tessa had let go of his hand and was haring towards it, waving and shouting. He saw the plane stop, and then Tessa clambered onto the wing and swung open the door. In a flash, she'd climbed inside.

There was a flicker of concern on the custom's officer's face. Was the plane going to take off again with the cocaine still aboard? But soon it was taxiing to the parking area.

It came to a final stop and the engine shut down. Tessa climbed out first and dropped to the ground, soon followed by her mother. Jason saw at once where Tessa got her good looks. Mrs Barrea's slim figure was shown to perfection in a stylish pair of jeans and a crisp white shirt. Her shiny hair was cut short, and when she took off her sunglasses Jason recognised Tessa's wide hazel eyes.

"Get the plane inside the hangar and out of view," commanded the airfield manager, signalling to the mechanics.

Once inside, Tessa's mother explained. "The cocaine's packed in the doors." She pointed out where the packets had been hidden. "And there's more in the fuselage behind the luggage area."

Like most of the planes in the race, the passenger seats had been removed to lighten the load. But with this plane, the weight had been replaced by cocaine.

They watched as the mechanics carefully dismantled the doors. Packed tightly inside were several packets of white powder. The custom's officer opened one of them and pressed his finger into the powder before putting it to his lips. "Cocaine all right," he pronounced. "We'll have to get the police in."

He turned to Jason and Tessa. "Looks like you kids are off the hook."

"Be careful when you open the fuselage," Mrs Barrea warned the mechanics. "The cocaine is packed round the controls." She supervised the operation to make sure none of the controls were damaged.

Tessa was grinning broadly at Jason. The next minute her arms slipped round his neck. "We did it, Jason. We outsmarted Raul."

He pulled her close, wishing they were alone. "We make a good team."

"The police will want your passport until all this is sorted out," said the custom's officer. "And they'll need statements."

"I think they can do that more comfortably at our house," said Mr Hunter, lifting Mrs Barrea's small case out of the luggage compartment. "I expect these two ladies will want to spend some time together."

Mrs Barrea flashed him a grateful smile. "That's very kind of you. Are you sure your wife won't mind you suddenly turning up with two strangers?"

"Oh, it won't be too sudden," Mr Hunter assured her. "Jason will be going on ahead to let her know. Won't you, son?" He lifted his eyebrows at Jason.

"Sure, Dad." Jason tried to keep the disappointment out of his voice. He had been planning to take Tessa back on the bike, and perhaps stop somewhere so they could be alone for a few minutes.

After a brief interview with the police he was walking back to the car park. Suddenly he spotted the tall figure of Raul. His eyes were blazing.

Mrs Hunter had the tea made and was cutting the sponge cake as her husband turned into the driveway.

"It doesn't seem right," she exclaimed, as the family filled her in with all the details and Mrs Barrea told them how she searched for Tessa. "D'you mean the police won't be able to charge the embassy staff with smuggling cocaine?"

"They won't be able to prosecute," explained Mr Hunter. "But I believe there will be a stern letter to the authorities in Argentina. I expect the entire staff will be recalled."

"And don't forget the two most important things," Jason reminded him. "We got Tessa out. And the police have the cocaine."

It wasn't long before they heard Caitlin's van drawing up.

"Oh, oh." Mr Hunter gave Jason a meaningful look. "You'd better do some quick talking to your sister."

Caitlin stormed in, followed by Mark, David, and Nicole. However, when she saw the two strangers sitting in the lounge drinking tea, it quite took the wind out of her sails.

"Caitlin, this is Samantha Barrea and her daughter, Tessa," said Mrs Hunter.

"Please call me Sam. No one's called me Samantha since my schooldays," said Mrs Barrea, laughing.

Then everyone seemed to be talking at once. David and Nicole wanted to know what had happened at the airfield, and Mark wondered whether there would be any sort of reward for finding the cocaine.

When the phone rang Mr Hunter went to answer it. "The police would like you to make a statement," he told Tessa's mother. "But they say they can wait until Monday."

Mrs Hunter insisted that Tessa and her mother stay for the weekend. "Jason won't mind sleeping on the couch. And Caitlin can have his room. You'll be much more comfortable in Caitlin's room," she told them.

Suddenly there were beds to be changed, and extra places set at the dining table. Caitlin offered to take Mark, David and Nicole home.

Once Jason had seen his friends off, he seized his chance. Taking Tessa's hand, he led her into the garden. Smoky clouds were drifting lazily across the moon. They strolled silently in the warm evening air towards the wooden bench set amongst the trees.

"What's that perfume?" asked Tessa, scenting the air.

Jason bent and picked up a yellowy pink flower that had drifted from the tree. "Frangipani."

She breathed in the scent. "It's beautiful."

"So are you," whispered Jason, taking her in his arms. When he kissed her, it was better than he'd ever dreamed. He wondered how long they would have together. "What will happen now? Will you go back to England with your mother?"

"I expect so."

"Can't you persuade her to stay for a while?"

"I doubt whether she'll have time." Her face was filled with regret. "She and her partner run a flying school."

"I wish she ran it here." He slipped his arm round her shoulders and they sat on the bench. "I've been trying to save for flying lessons."

"Perhaps you can persuade your parents to let you come to England for the next holidays."

Jason was doubtful. The flight alone would be more than he could afford. Perhaps his father would give him a loan. He looked into Tessa's expectant face. He could always sell his scrambler. It would be worth it. "I'll ask them," he finally said.

Caitlin's van swept into the driveway. "Come on," said Jason. "We'd better help with the supper or Caitlin will never forgive me."

"Oh, there you are," said Mrs Hunter as Jason and Tessa walked into the kitchen. "I've just been talking to Sam. D'you know they live quite close to your Aunt Vera. We were saying, wouldn't it be nice if you could go over and stay with Vera for the next holidays."

"Yes," put in Mr Hunter. "Sam says she can get you a discount on the flight. What d'you think?"

Grinning, Jason turned to Tessa. They exchanged smiles before bursting into laughter.

Later that night, Jason lay on the couch listening to the murmur of voices upstairs. It was hard to believe that Tessa was actually in his house. So much had happened since the day he fell off his bike and first saw her.

Drowsily he re-lived the events. Mark's initial scepticism; the dinner-party on the sugar estate where he'd learned about the embassy's reception; the fight on the beach - he could feel again the adrenaline rush as Tessa's uncle's fist lunged towards his face; the stomach-churning fear when the chopper carrying the radio was caught in an up-draft and almost hit the eaves. So many things could have gone wrong. He almost broke into a sweat when he recalled their flight in the Beechcraft. Another few minutes in the air and he and Tessa would have been history when the fuel ran out.

There was a soft chuckle of laughter from upstairs. What was he worrying about? Tessa was safe, and tomorrow they would have the whole day together. He began planning what they would do. Take her to the beach - maybe she'd like to try surfing. And there was always the conservation area close-by with its secluded walks. Smiling, he snuggled down under the covers anticipating the pleasures tomorrow would bring.

CPSIA information can be obtained
at www.ICGtesting.com
Printed in the USA
LVOW04s1330060216
473994LV00025B/941/P